Hope you enjoy my 'little story'!
Des

UPON THE HEARTH A BLESSING

A Novel by D. Berkana Tiwari

Acknowledgements

I want to thank my family and friends for their support and encouragement to pursue my writing. I am especially grateful to my dear friend, Newfoundland artist Julie Duff, who also read early pages and kept me motivated to finish the story.

For Linda

Upon The Hearth A Blessing

Copyright © 2016 D. Berkana Tiwari

Chapter 1 – In the Name of Friendship

As the plane slid down through the clouds, Helen caught glimpses of the rugged beauty of the Scottish coastline. Steep rocks stood sentinel against an aggressive sea, with the bright green of plant life snaking in and around the grey formations to provide a striking contrast. The country from this angle appeared austere and unwelcoming in spite of its awe inspiring beauty. Approaching the Glasgow airport, the topography changed quickly to rolling hills dotted with farms, and then to the red rooftops of urban development.

Helen buckled her seatbelt and braced herself for landing. She hated flying – especially taking-off and landing. *Don't look out the window,* she thought to herself as the pilot turned the plane steeply before going in for the final approach. *If I look out the window I will be sick. Come on, come on...land this sucker.* There was a minor bump as the rear landing gear hit the runway, and then a final bigger thud as the front came down. This was the worst part for Helen. When she let go of the armrests, her hands were covered in sweat. *Four weeks to the next flight. Thank god. I actually made it.*

Helen did not know why she was so afraid of flying when she was practically fearless in other aspects of her life. It wasn't a fear of death. As a medical student, she had examined a number of cadavers and body parts in medical school, and had felt awe and fascination with the human anatomy. A dedicated doctor, her focus was on saving lives or, preventing disease, and, in the case of untreatable illnesses, finding treatments to make living bearable for her patients. Although focused on doing everything in her power to keep patients alive, her pragmatic view of death held that it was, after all, the inevitable conclusion of a human lifecycle, whether from old age, incurable disease or accident. Her decision to go beyond a physician's practice to focus on cancer research meant working closely with one of the most frightening and lethal diseases known to mankind. Perhaps, for Helen, it was more of a fear of losing control over a situation that caused her anxiety when flying. In the lab, she controlled the context and the activity within it. On a plane, she could control very little and only put her trust in the crew and hope for the best. Thank goodness her family and friends understood this, even if it perplexed them to do so. She had missed many important events and occasions with family and friends because of her unwillingness to get on a plane.

Hence, this trip to Scotland was long overdue. There were no family ties here, so to speak, but Sarah had lived here for almost eight years and, in that time, Helen hadn't been over to see her even once. They were best friends – lifelong friends since the age of three. They had been almost inseparable until Sarah met Ian Wallace when they were in graduate school at university. It was love at first sight for Sarah; something Helen couldn't understand since she did not find Ian appealing in any way. However, despite the friends' previous similar views on what comprised the 'man-you-would-have-children-with' profile, Sarah and Ian became a couple, made it legal a year after they met, and then Sarah went home with him to Scotland.

Helen had been dismayed that Sarah had gone before finishing her own program. She thought it was unfair that just because Ian's doctorate was finished and he had a job offer at the University of Aberdeen, that Sarah dropped her professional goals and plans to return with him to begin a completely new kind of life. It really had all taken place too quickly in Helen's estimation. Sarah resisted her cautions against marrying Ian without living with him for awhile first to test the relationship, or without having ever visited

Scotland with him, as opposed to going back with him as his wife. Helen had heard about too much unhappiness resulting from these kinds of situations before from other young women she had known at school who had married foreign students. She wanted to be sure that her Sarah would be happy.

In the end, it came down to losing their friendship or supporting Sarah in the life she had chosen for herself. It was no contest; the friendship was too deep, too much a part of Helen. And yet, except for the visits that Sarah made to see her own family in Toronto, they really hadn't spent a lot of time together over the past several years. Sure, they had visited on those trips, but Sarah had been swamped with, first one, and then two, babies to look after, along with visiting relatives and friends who were anxious to see her and meet her little ones. There had been baptisms in Canada for both boys, and Ian had accompanied Sarah for those trips. While Helen had, of course, been invited, and helped out tremendously with those events, she and Sarah had few opportunities for any of their in-depth conversations. So, Helen and Sarah had kept in touch by phone, text and e-mail mostly, and, more recently, by skype. They each seemed to sense when the other needed to talk, and one or the other would call or text at just the right time.

Helen sensed from the start that Ian wasn't all that keen on their friendship, perhaps because it was so important to both women to maintain it. Maybe he felt threatened by Helen - that she might usurp some of Sarah's time. He wanted her all to himself, that was pretty clear from the beginning. He had grudgingly accepted their 'one-day-a-week' exclusive time to spend together when they were still at university. Helen had always secretly suspected that his eagerness to return to Scotland was at least partly due to his not so veiled jealousy of their relationship. He wanted Sarah's attention focused on him and only him, which was, in part, what Helen didn't like about him. He seemed too insular and she feared he might be controlling. Not that he had ever overtly indicated that he didn't like Helen, or that he didn't want Sarah to spend time with her. It was just something that Helen sensed, and she felt that Sarah knew this too. So, in the name of friendship, Helen backed off and fit herself into Sarah's life as it suited Sarah and Ian. She knew Sarah appreciated that this was an effort for her, and, if anything, it solidified their friendship and made it stronger. Now Helen was in Scotland to visit them. Sarah's two boys, Jonah was seven and Nathan had just turned five, had been joined by a baby sister a few months ago. Sarah had asked Helen to be the baby's godmother at the baptism, planned for the Sunday after Helen's arrival. The baby would be christened "Helen Sarah Wallace". The birth of this baby had brought Helen, finally, to visit her childhood friend in Scotland.

Helen looked anxiously around the Glasgow airport baggage area for Sarah. She hadn't seen her for almost two years, and wondered if she had changed much. The last time Sarah was over to Canada, she'd looked tired and a bit too thin. Her usually glowing complexion had been replaced by a paleness that seemed to Helen to border on anemia. She had been concerned about her friend. Sarah's state of mind had been consistent with her physical appearance as well. She wasn't her exuberant, happy-go-lucky self. Instead, she seemed introspective and exhausted. She'd laughed it off when Helen expressed concern, saying that looking after two kids, a house and a husband was the hardest work she'd ever done, and that she was just plain tired. But there was something else, Helen knew it; some reason for the lack of life in Sarah's once brilliant blue eyes and glorious curly brown hair. She used to glow and seemed a mere shadow of her former self. But, once again, Helen had kept her real theories to herself on the reason for Sarah's change in appearance.

She remembered when they had just begun university – how wonderfully alive they both were, unfettered with responsibilities or significant relationships. Sarah was an absolute beauty with a vibrant, outgoing personality. She drew people to her like there was an invisible magnet – everyone loved her. Helen, on the other hand, was less popular, especially among the "in" crowd. She had an aura of quiet intelligence about her and she was softspoken. She was not a wallflower – far from it. There was a persistence about her that could inspire awe in even the most pedantic of professors. Her angelic, white-blonde looks belied a devilish ability to latch onto a topic, research it into oblivion, and challenge anyone who dared to venture an opinion without being fully versed in the subject matter.

It may have been this intellectual intensity, visible in her clear green eyes that struck fear into the men who had ventured to ask her out, and then failed to call again after one or two dates. Helen was puzzled by this and not sure how to remedy the situation. She was herself with everyone and did not undergo the personality change she observed in other women when an eligible man entered the room. She stood firm in her conviction that she would not be reduced to some sort of ridiculous mating ritual just to have a relationship with someone. She had not yet come across her intellectual equal, or, even more than that, someone who was smart and confident enough in himself to appreciate the combination of brains and beauty and not feel threatened by it. As a result, this meant she was alone most of the time. This state of affairs saddened her, although only Sarah knew how much. Sarah had kept telling her to lighten-up a bit, but she didn't know how to do that. She admired Sarah's ability to walk into any room and liven it up. Sarah was a bit of a flirt and could manage to subdue her intelligence in social situations. Not that she acted stupidly or anything; she just seemed to have that knack for having fun and being lively around the opposite sex – listening attentively to what they said as if it was ground-breaking news, and keeping whatever might be her real thoughts to herself. Sarah was very smart, but she believed in saving it for when she was working – a firm believer in "All work and no play makes Jill a dull girl". That's what it all boiled down to in Helen's mind; Sarah was right—but Helen just didn't know how to play, or she couldn't remember; it looked like she would have to settle for a life dedicated to work.

Sarah spotted Helen sitting on a bench in the baggage terminal, her precisely placed suitcases in front of her as if there as a barrier between her and the masses. She was a half-hour late in getting to the airport and carried her sleeping baby snuggled against her breasts in one of those front kangaroo-type pouch carriers. She chuckled to herself knowingly as she approached Helen, who hadn't seen her yet. *She hasn't changed a bit,* she thought to herself. *She looks tired, but, god, how can she still look so young?* Sarah herself felt quite haggard and in need of about three days' solid sleep. Looking at Helen sitting there alone reminded Sarah of the first time she'd seen her when they were both small children. Helen had been sitting on the front steps of her house in exactly the same position as she was now with various toys and dolls surrounding her as if to provide protection from the world beyond. There was a look of sadness on her pretty, but small, pale face that Sarah would always remember because she was struck by it at the time. Sarah had skipped up to her new neighbour's house and plunked herself down beside the little blonde girl and stared at her with her own sparkling blue eyes.

Little Helen had seem surprised at this onslaught and physically withdrew into her fortress of toys. But Sarah's energy and charisma, even at the tender age of three, warmed Helen to her once Sarah began chattering with her about her dolls and asked Helen to come and play with her in her house while Helen's parents finished sorting out the house. They were fast friends from that day on, and as they grew into young women, the relationship deepened as, together, they experienced the joys and challenges of growing up.

Sarah had her own theories, which she kept to herself, on why Helen was such a serious person and, with the exception of their friendship, almost reclusive. Naturally, their respective parents had gotten to know each other because the girls became close friends, although they never really went beyond the level of polite social conversation. Helen's parents were nice if a bit aloof; they loved their daughter, that was plain to see, but they were intent on her achieving success in everything she did. As a child, Helen had an enviable number of expensive toys and dolls, but not much of an opportunity to play with them unless Sarah was over. There were always so many activities and lessons that Helen had to attend, and not much play time. This lack of leisure time persisted until both young women left home after graduating from highschool.

Sarah, on the other hand, was allowed to choose her activities, and her home was always open to friends for unrestricted shenanigans. Even though she too was an only child, the house was always full of people and noise – the pleasant noise of people enjoying themselves. Helen loved going to Sarah's house, although she was in awe of the constant activity over there, and, at times, overwhelmed by the energy level of its occupants. She liked to observe more than participate, except when she and Sarah were involved in a game or making something together. As much as she did like it at Sarah's house, she was usually glad to return to the quiet sanctity of her own home. She knew that Sarah found it boring at her house because they had to be quiet so as not to disturb Helen's father who spent much of his time working in his study. The Brooks liked children, as long as they weren't rambunctious, so they insisted on non-disruptive-to-the-house activities. Sarah expected that when they both moved out to their own apartment together, that Helen would breathe a sigh of relief and relax. But instead, she loaded-up her time with organized activities to the near exclusion of any social interaction or events. Sarah always had to drag her to parties and dances, only to look around later in the evening to discover that Helen had slipped out and gone home. Sarah wished Helen would make more of an effort to enjoy herself and be sociable, but she accepted Helen as she was and certainly the two of them had fun when they were together. Helen's barriers went down around Sarah and she relaxed. Really, their only point of contention, sometimes, was the noise level in their apartment and the number of visitors at a given time. Helen required peace and tranquility and, of course, Sarah coveted the opposite. So, they agreed to some house rules regarding these issues and, for the most part, got along famously. They were loyal friends and appreciated each other's abilities and very different personalities.

    Helen looked up from her watch to meet the gaze of a familiar pair of blue eyes. She jumped up to give her dear Sarah a hug and realized Sarah was carrying the baby. She stopped to look at the tiny, sweet face and tears sprang to her eyes. "Oh Sari, she's lovely," murmured Helen as she stared at the glossy black curls and eyebrows of the sleeping child. The baby's small, red lips formed a crooked smile and she looked perfectly content. "I'm so happy to be here for the baptism, and to see you. It's been too long." She carefully hugged Sarah again and kissed her on both cheeks.

"Me too, Lenny, me too." Sarah replied, invoking the pet name that had developed because, at the age of three, she had found the name 'Helen" a bit of a tongue twister. Sarah looked happily at her friend. She seemed to light up and some of the sparkle returned to her eyes. She felt less tired suddenly, as if a weight had been lifted from her. "You have no idea how glad I am to see you. I've been looking forward to this for weeks-no months….ever since the baby was born. As soon as I saw her, I told Ian we had to ask you to be her Godmother and namesake. Not that I hadn't thought of it before, but it just seem imperative as soon as she opened her eyes. Oh, but you know how I am! Speaking of the baptism, there is so much to do this week. I'm afraid I haven't been too organized, Lenny. It's really just going to be a family affair and small and simple. I don't have the energy for a party! Things have changed, Lenny." Sarah prattled on jumping from topic to topic, and Helen felt as if they'd never been apart. She listened contentedly to Sarah chatter about the state of affairs in the Wallace household as they walked to the car, and it was obvious that Sarah was ecstatic to have her there.

They were home before the boys came in from school. The baby had slept all the way from the Glasgow airport to Aberdeenshire, which was about a two hour drive, and was now awake as she was cuddled in Helen's arms. She was a beautiful child and looked very much like her mother so far, having inherited Sarah's blue eyes and dark hair. She was fair in complexion, though, like Ian.

"You're not going to call her 'Lenny' are you?" asked Helen as she played with the baby's tiny toes.

"No," laughed Sarah, busy in the kitchen preparing dinner. "There's only one Lenny in this world and that's you. You know that." She winked at Helen as she deftly folded a pile of towels while she waited for the Aga oven to heat up. "Although I do hope she will somehow pattern herself after you rather than me. I want her to be focused and independent, not scattered and needy like me!"

"What on earth do you mean?" asked Helen, surprised at her friend's self-deprecation. Sarah had always been so confident and sure of herself. "Don't say that about yourself. You've never been scattered or needy. For heaven's sake Sari, how can you even think that?"

"Oh well, I've changed, Lenny. Ian's always telling me how disorganized I am. And he is right. I can't seem to complete the simplest task. I don't know what happened to my brain cells when I gave birth, but I'll warn you now – don't expect much in the way of stimulating conversation from me. All I seem to be able to talk about are my children."

"Look here, Sari," began Helen, about to get straight to the point in her usual way. "I want to hear about your children and what they do and say; that's why I am here – to see you and the children. Believe me, holding this baby, your baby, right now is the most wonderful thing I've done in a long time. So there. And furthermore, Ian shouldn't be telling you anything of the sort. Disorganized indeed! I'd like to see him look after the children and keep this house in order the way you obviously have. And I'll be happy to tell him so!"

"Oh no, Lenny – please don't do that. I want you two to get along. If possible. Please. I think he's feeling a little neglected or something; you know how he was if I spent time with you or anyone else. He's been kind of like that since the kids came along. He loves them dearly but he needs attention too, only, I'm just too bloody tired these days. By the time I finish the day, I fall into bed and sleep. I can't even stay up to watch the news with him. It's hard on him, sweetie."

Helen bit her tongue and cooed at the baby while Sarah continued to prepare dinner and set the table. *Hard on him my butt. What a throwback. How could Sarah have ended-up with such a jerk. He obviously doesn't realize how fortunate he is – he never did. Sarah could have had her pick of any number of great guys and she picked him. He's bloody lucky. He needs to grow up.* "I'll behave myself with Ian, Sarah. I'm not here to create stress for you; I'm here to help. What can I do?" Helen strapped the baby in her activity chair. At that moment the door flew open and two boys eagerly rushed in to greet her.

"Aunt Lenny! Aunt Lenny! You are here!" cried Jonah, going straight to Helen for a big hug and kiss. Nathan stopped just short of Helen and waited; he was a little shy but clearly excited to see her. Helen grabbed him next and drew him close for his hugs and kisses too. They were glowing with health, and their ruddy cheeks belied the cool air of the Scottish highlands. Helen took them upstairs to her room and pulled out some shopping bags from her suitcase – one for each of them. Wide-eyed, they opened the bags and drew out some red hoodies with Canadian Mounties on them, and some Canada t-shirts and hats. Helen had always provided them with these every year and they loved them. She had also checked with colleagues who had boys their ages to see what was the current desired toy, and she brought each of them the latest version of an electronic toy along with a half dozen games. When the boys saw those, they jumped on her and she was treated to more hugs and kisses. Sarah appeared in the doorway with the baby and smiled as she watched Helen and the boys.

"You are too generous, Lenny; you're spoiling them."

"That is my job as their honourary aunt, right boys?" They enthusiastically agreed with her and dashed off to their room with loot in hand, anxious to try out their new games. "Honestly, Sarah, it's so much fun to bring them treats, and they are so polite – you've really done a fantastic job with them. Some of the kids I see at home are such ruffians – no manners – rude, loud, demanding – it's unbelievable. These guys are a breath of fresh air!"

Sarah smiled at her friend, knowing that even if her boys were ruffian-like in their behaviour, which was inevitable, Helen would likely not mind because she loved them unconditionally, and this had always been the case. Her boys could do no wrong in their auntie Lenny's eyes, and were held up as an example, however unfair it might be, to all other boys of the same age she happened to encounter. She could not be more loyal or loving if she had been Sarah's blood sister and the boys' real aunt. And, of course, Helen saw them once a year at best, and the time was precious to her so she spoiled them rotten and completely interfered if anyone attempted to discipline them in her presence. Sarah didn't mind this at all and was rather amused by it, but Ian would get annoyed. Sarah sensed that annoying Ian was a motivator for Helen and she would indulge the boys' antics especially when Ian was about.

Later that night, as Helen lay in bed watching the fire die down in the bedroom fireplace, she thought about the evening's events. After dinner, and after the boys had finished their homework, played a bit of "footy", as they called soccer, and then gone to bed, she and Sarah sat down to organize the preparations for the baptism on Sunday. Sarah hadn't been joking when she said she'd only been able to get the invitations out, and they were mostly to Ian's family and a few close friends. Helen was the only visitor from Canada, as Sarah's parents couldn't make it and planned to visit later in the year. Sarah was swamped with the cares of a new baby, in addition to all of her other work as a wife and mother, and she was bone-tired, looking pale and drawn. Ian was working late most nights, as he had on this night, and was unable to contribute much to the planning. Helen quickly surmised the situation and determined what needed to be done, writing out the tasks on lists. At least the church preparations were made, with the exception of the Reverend's meeting with the godparents to discuss their responsibility as such. While they had only four days to finalize arrangements, now that Helen was there, it seemed manageable. She saw the look of relief on Sarah's face when what had seemed impossible to get done was now a nicely organized set of tasks to be accomplished on each of the next four days. It was to be a simple gathering at their home to celebrate the naming of their child and her baptism in the church where Wallaces had been baptized for generations. Helen determined that she would also see to it that Sarah got some rest during her visit, as much as Helen could facilitate for her dear Sarah. As the fire went down and the room darkened, Helen fell into a deep sleep, snuggled comfortably into the down mattress and cozy beside the fireplace.

Chapter 2 - A Disturbing Experience

A chilly sensation on her right hand roused Helen from her sleep. She turned groggily onto her side to look down at her hand which was dangling off the bed over the hearth of the fireplace. Startled, her eyes widened in horror at what she saw. A tiny white hand reached out of the fireplace and grasped Helen's fingers and then as much of her hand as it could manage. The arm seemed to come from beneath the tiles and the little hand held tightly to her's. Helen cried out in alarm, but still the hand held on. It wasn't pulling her hand, but, rather, hanging on to it as if wanting to be pulled from the hearth. Helen screamed, "Let go! Let go. Let me go!" She could not loosen her hand from its hold; the small hand persisted and possessed an incredible strength as it grasped Helen's hand even more tightly. Helen was terrified. The more she pulled, the tighter the grasp. The hand was like ice and the feel of it sent a chill through Helen's body like an electric shock. "Please let go of my hand" Helen begged, "please. Let go…let go!" She seemed to have no strength of her own to move, as if she was paralyzed. A feeling of fear knotted her stomach and a sense of tremendous dread overwhelmed her.

She could not take her eyes off of this little hand – a child's hand. It was so pale, a kind of whitish-grey, and attached to a tiny arm reaching up out of the tiles. She could not see a body, but felt its existence through the tension in the hand. It was intent on being pulled out, or so it seemed, holding onto Helen as if it wanted her help in releasing it from the hearth. This struggle continued for what seemed like hours. She could hear herself crying out, and then was suddenly aware that she must be dreaming. How could she extract herself from this horrible nightmare? With a tremendous effort, as if she was battling some force holding her down, Helen suddenly wrenched her hand free and sat up in the bed.

"Lenny, what's the matter?" An obviously alarmed Sarah stood beside Helen's bed. "Are you all right? You were moaning quite loudly. I was checking on baby and heard you from the hall."

Helen quickly looked at the fireplace; there was no fire or anything else. The hearth tiles were undisturbed and reflected the moonlight coming in from the window. She was shaking, covered in perspiration and breathing heavily. "I guess I've had a nightmare….I'm sorry I woke you up" she said, her voice trembling. "I hope I didn't wake the children or the baby."

"No, just me, Helen." A deep voice said from the darkness of the hall. Ian emerged into the room from the doorway. "I was going to wait for you in the morning to give you a proper welcome, but I guess I don't have to now. Since we're all awake." The latter comment had a rather accusing tone to it.

"Ian. I am so sorry" stammered Helen, feeling defensive, "what a nuisance to have your guest wake you up with a nightmare. I'm sure it's that flight over – you know how afraid I am of flying, combined with the jetlag, indigestion and surly flight attendants – you know how it is. Anyway, it's good to be here, but what a way to get reacquainted!" Helen tried to rally herself out of a defensive embarrassment she was certain Ian would relish.

"And we are glad to have you. We've all been looking forward to your arrival. Especially Sarah, of course. Sarah, let's get back to bed. The baby will be up in a couple of hours, and I need my sleep. Good night Helen – I hope the demons have left and you can sleep. I'll see you tomorrow evening." With that, Ian abruptly turned and left the room.

Helen felt foolish and annoyed that Ian had used the opportunity to greet her when she was at a disadvantage. *He hasn't changed a bit. He could have had the decency to wait until tomorrow to see me. My ass he's glad I'm here. He needs his sleep? That's a laugh. Poor Sarah-she's the one who needs some sleep. What a jerk!* Sarah had plumped Helen's pillows and smoothed the covers for her. "Listen, you go back to sleep. The children make a lot of noise when they get up and I daresay they will wake you. Are you sure you're alright? It must have been some dream! Who were you yelling at to "let go"?

"I'm fine, Sari. Sorry about this. I really feel badly that I woke Ian and scared you."

"Never mind Lenny; I am pretty sure he was more or less awake anyway – he hasn't been sleeping that well himself. And, so what? It's not the end of the world, is it? Quit apologizing. I just hope you get a good rest now. You'll have to tell me about your dream tomorrow. Goodnight." Sarah tucked the covers around Helen, as she would a child, smiled, and left the room.

"Goodnight, and thanks Sari. See you in the morning." Helen was exhausted, but still troubled by the dream she had. *It was so real. I was sure I was awake-I could feel the hand. But it must have been a dream-Sarah woke you up...* After some further musings of this nature, she drifted off into a deep and peaceful sleep.

Chapter 3 – Friends and Family

Helen's eyes opened to see two sets of mischievous eyes staring back at her. The boys were dressed in their school uniforms, with their hair neatly slicked down. Jonah, the eldest, was a real combination of his parents. He had straight auburn hair like Ian, a medium complexion like Sarah, and her sparkling blue eyes. He was slender, but well proportioned. Nathan looked like Ian, except for his hair and eyes. They were Sarah's eyes with a slight hazel cast. His hair was curly like his Mom's, but he had Ian's fair skin and muscular build. Both of them were going to be tall like their parents. They emanated health and happiness. Jonah was lively and exuberant, while Nathan was more reserved and followed his brother's lead. Both of them loved their Aunt Lenny dearly.

"Here's your coffee, Aunty" said Jonah, struggling to balance the large cup and saucer. "Mummy said to bring it in and set it down on the table but not to wake you up. But we wanted to say goodbye before we left for school." They both had the upper-crust Scottish accent of their father.

Helen threw back the duvet and swung her feet to the floor. She took the coffee from Jonah and set it down on the night table. Then she drew both boys close in a big hug. "I am so glad you did. I couldn't have a great day without seeing my two best fellows, now could I?" She laughed as they giggled. "But now, you know – I can't have any kisses. Absolutely no kisses. You know I don't like them." With that encouragement, the boys began kissing her cheeks as she pretended to be horrified. There were shrieks of delight and rough-housing as they tumbled around on the bed.

"Boys, boys! Jonah-stop that! Nathan!" Sarah rushed into the room with the baby in one arm. "I thought I told you not to wake her up."

"Sorry, Mummy, but she made us kiss her!" exclaimed Nathan, with a grin that stretched from ear to ear.

"Oh. I see," laughed Sarah. "It was the old – I don't like to be kissed- ploy, was it?" Helen and the boys giggled. "Oh look! Baby is smiling! Look everybody!" As if in on the joke too, little Helen Sarah had a funny, crooked smile on her face as if on the verge of a good laugh. They all chuckled to see it, and gathered around Sarah to marvel at the sweet little girl.

After the boys left for school, Helen and Sarah went over the lists they had prepared the night before. They determined that many of the tasks could be accomplished over the phone and proceeded to the lists for the shopping that needed doing. The reception at the house would be simple, but elegant. After church, everyone would come back to the house for champagne and strawberries, followed by high tea, and the opening of the gifts. They decided to go into Aberdeen for the champagne, and to order the cake and tea pastries from the new French pastisserie. Sarah had already asked her housecleaner to prepare the little sandwiches; she was originally from London and had surprised Sarah once with a lovely tea, so Sarah commissioned her to prepare an English high tea for this occasion. All Sarah and Helen had to do was to shop for the ingredients. Sarah made calls to the florist and the church while Helen looked after the baby. Already many items on the lists were completed, and Sarah relaxed and began to enjoy herself.

Once they had lunch, they bundled the little one into her car seat and drove the ten kilometers into the city. The baby fell asleep almost immediately, while Helen admired the neatly tended fields dotted with sheep and the odd cow.

"I forgot to ask you this morning," began Sarah, "what were you dreaming about last night? You looked really frightened." As Helen told her about the dream, Sarah shivered.

"I hope I'm not scaring you, Sari. It was just a dream after all. It did give me a fright though – it was so real." She hesitated for a moment, and then went on. "Sari-the house. Who lived there before?"

"Oh. You really mean, who died there, don't you?" Sarah returned, smiling. "Rest easy – nobody did. The fellow who built the house sold it to us. He died a few years ago in a hospital – of old age." She went on. "You know, you should talk to Ian's brother, Matty, about your dream. He's quite spiritual, and interested in things like that. Anyway, you'll see him tonight; he's coming for dinner, and he'll probably stay over."

"What's he like, Sari?" Helen imagined the worst. *Great. Another Ian to contend with. I hope he's not a pompous ass like his brother.*

"Honestly, Lenny, I think you will like him. He's so nice, and he has been so good to me and the children. Really good. There when we needed him. The boys love him to bits. He's not really much like Ian personality-wise in that he seems to need to be with other people – it is quite endearing, really. He is a gentle soul, and just as quiet as Ian, but sociable, and when he's had a few pints he can be quite engaging and entertaining.

Well, this sounds promising, but I'll believe it when I see it. "I'll look forward to meeting him, Sari, it does seem odd that we've never managed to meet before."

"He's a sweetheart-really," coaxed Sarah, sensing the skepticism in Helen's response. "Anyway, you should talk to him about this dream. He's a bit of a bedside psychologist; maybe he can figure out whether it means anything or not. Actually, he's offered to take you about for a bit of sightseeing while you are here."

"That's nice of him – what a good idea." *Wonderful. I will be trapped in a car for hours with Ian's brother.*

They finished their shopping early enough to stop by the boys' school to surprise them with a ride home. Helen was playing football with them in the yard when a grey Mercedes pulled into the drive and honked twice. Jonah and Nathan immediately stopped playing and ran over to the car as a tall, fair man with dark brown hair got out.

"Uncle Matty, Uncle Matty! Do you want to play football with us?" They obviously loved the man and jumped all over him. He didn't seem to mind. He looked at Helen and she recognized his eyes. Although they were hazel, they were the same as Ian's.

"You must be Helen Brooks," he said, after hugging the boys and roughing-up their hair. "I am Matthew Wallace; your better half for the christening." He winked at her and offered his hand.

"It's nice to finally meet you, Matthew. I am really happy to be here and I am thrilled Ian and Sarah asked me to be Helen-Sarah's godmother. Now, what was that about the better half? I am not so sure about that!" *He's a bit forward, but at least he's not a stiff like his brother. He actually seems friendly. Why did I have to say anything about the better half remark? He was trying to be funny Helen-you nitwit.*

"Nor should you be. I am lucky to be asked to be godfather, given that I'm a bit of a disappointment to the family-namely-Ian. Haven't quite lived up to his expectations – or maybe I have, actually. Really, I'm rather shocked that they asked me. Especially given that you are the *other* half – how's that? Oh, and call me Matty – everyone in the family does."

Helen was embarrassed. *Stuck your foot in it again didn't you? Making friends and influencing people as ususal. Get yourself out of this one.* "Oh, I was just kidding – a poor attempt to match your wit. I really haven't heard that much about you." *Oh god- that came out wrong. He must think I'm a complete idiot now.*

"No, I'm quite sure you haven't heard much about me from my brother. I don't think he likes to talk about me too much. But you – I have heard about all of your accomplishments over the years. Quite the scientist, I hear. Ian tells me that you won a couple of prestigious research awards last year. You'll have to tell me more about it. Breast cancer research, I think?"

"Oh, yes – sure" stammered Helen, completely taken by surprise that Ian had spoken about this. Just then Sarah appeared with the baby, and Ian arrived in his car. Matty went to Sarah and took the baby from her. As he cradled the infant in his lean, muscular arms, Helen was amazed by the absolute gentleness with which he held her – as if she was the most precious, fragile thing he had ever touched. Helen turned her gaze to Sarah, and, as she did, their eyes met. Sarah's glinted slyly, and she lifted one eyebrow. Helen laughed to herself because she recognized an old signal they used with each other to denote the discovery of what they then termed a "desirable specimen". *I think she has more in mind for Matthew and me than a distant link as godparents. I should have known.* Helen frowned at Sarah and then they both immediately broke into giggles.

"Did I do something amusing?" asked Matty.

"Don't get them laughing, brother," Ian's voice asserted itself, cutting like a knife through their laughter. "We'll never get any dinner if you do!"

"Aye, Ian. Now that would be tragic." He noticed the hurt look on Sarah's face. "I think we should take matters into our able hands and make dinner-just to make sure it's done right. Sarah and Helen can entertain the boys – we'll take little Helen to help us in the kitchen." Helen bit her lips to keep from making a sarcastic comment. Ian frowned and he grunted an agreement. He and Matty went into the house.

"Thank you, Lenny."

"For what, Sari?"

"For not taking the bait from Ian. I could see he was hoping for a reaction from you."

"Was he? Or is he always like this with you, Sari? Honestly, does he think you are here to wait on him? For god's sake, you are more than his intellectual equal!"

"Oh-let's not go down that road again, Lenny. Right now, and for a good several years more, I've got three children to nurture. It's what I want to do, and I need every drop of energy I have to do it the way I think it needs to be done. It's the hardest but most rewarding work I have ever done-including my Ph.D. research!"

"I'm sorry. I know. I am not trying to diminish what you are doing. I think you are the best mother I have ever seen. I admire you for it. Maybe I am a little bit jealous too. I will never have this – I know it. I repel every man I spend time with-it's a gift."

"Now, Lenny-you're not like that. I know you are just looking out for me. But you don't have to. Ian is really very good to me; he just gets nervous around you. He always has, and we both know he's always been a bit jealous of you. He requires a lot of attention, but I do love him. Come on, let's go play with the boys. I haven't run around playing football for weeks!" With that, they joined the two rosy-cheeked boys in a rousing game.

After dinner, and once the dishes had been cleared away, and children bathed and put to bed, Sarah, Helen and the two brothers settled down in front of a vigorous fire with glasses of some local whisky. Sarah lit candles around the living room and turned out the lights, and it seemed to Helen to be perhaps the most peaceful place she had been in a long time. The whisky didn't hurt either. Even Ian was relaxed and cracked the odd smile at something his brother said. The wind was quite forceful that night and the sound of it could be heard from time to time – which made the room seem more cozy and warm.

"Matt-feel free to spend the night here – the wind is pretty strong tonight," said Sarah, who noticed how much her brother-in-law seemed to be enjoying himself.

"If it's not putting you to any trouble, Sarah, I'd love to. Frankly, I've had a bit too much to drink to set out now, and I am pretty damned comfortable in this chair right now. Cheers," he replied, looking at Ian for a sign that he approved of this.

"Aye, stay with us. You're always welcome here – you know that. I think my wife prefers your sunny disposition to mine anyway, brother." This was Ian's agreement to his wife's invitation. He was happy to have his brother stay; he loved him dearly. If only he would do something serious with his life. Matt was pushing forty and, in Ian's mind, really hadn't settled down to any serious occupation as yet. He had taken a law degree at Edinburgh fifteen years before, but had never done his articles or practiced. Instead, he spent his time painting landscapes – abstract landscapes. He had begun painting the landscapes as a way to relax during his studies at law school, but it became more than that after a time, and people had taken an interest in his paintings.

Ian didn't like anything abstract, particularly art, but Matt seemed to have found a market for these paintings of his all over the U.K. Or rather, the market found him. In fact, Matt's paintings of Scottish landscapes sold like haggis on Robby Burns' day. Granted, he made a decent living from it, and along with the money from his trust fund, he was set financially; however, Ian wasn't sure that this could be truly classified as a career. Yet, when he looked at his brother's happy countenance and easy-going attitude, there was a definite twinge in Ian's belly. Perhaps he was the one who had missed out on life's pleasures by working so hard at something he loved, but was usually a solitary pursuit. There was, albeit, great satisfaction in having an article published in a peer-reviewed journal, but not much attention paid beyond a few notes of congratulations from his colleagues. Certainly there were no cocktail parties or grand openings at trendy galleries. Not that Ian liked these types of affairs much anyway, having attended some because he was the artist's brother, but he did take notice of the attention Matt received – much of it from gushing women.

Ian had always worked at one thing or another despite the family's reasonably comfortable status. His father had stressed the importance of both, what he termed, 'a good day's work', and ensuring what was already in the bank was being added to and earning interest. As a small boy, Ian had his chores around the small estate, whether it be helping the gardener or carrying the bank books for his father when he made his monthly trek to the bank to check on the status of accounts and investments. It was then Ian's job to observe and learn, and to return the books to their proper place when they got home. He took these tasks seriously, and put his best effort forward in order to please his father. Perhaps it was the untimely death of their father when Matt was just fifteen that precluded Matt's heading in the same direction as Ian. Ian really didn't think so though, as Matt just simply was never interested – he had a different nature. From the time he was a toddler, Matt was very easy-going and delighted in just existing, it seemed, especially if that meant finger-painting or lying on his back on a hill and gazing at the clouds. He wasn't interested in being taught numbers or letters and laughed when Ian would try to make him do so. And they all, including Ian, loved the cheerful little fellow, and pretty much let him grow up as he wished, perhaps spoiling him a bit too much at times. Except for his choice of career, Matt seemed to be managing quite well, although he did rely on Ian to handle the finances of the family trust fund.

Ian watched his three companions in the firelight and liked what he saw. Sarah looked so beautiful, but so tired. He felt a bit guilty about that. With the faculty cuts at the university, classes had grown to unheard of numbers, and unless he spent at least three or four hours every evening marking papers and preparing lectures, he simply could not keep up.

He sensed that Helen still did not approve of him, which made him nervous around her. He was sure that he was always saying the wrong thing. He recalled saying and doing some pretty dumb things when they were all at university, but he always felt like the proverbial fifth wheel when Helen was around. She monopolized Sarah's attention and stared daggers at him when he tried to get a word in edgewise. He wasn't quite sure how to set things right between them, or even if it was possible. He surmised that some of what divided them was cultural. Scottish women were aggressive and kept their men close, but they knew their place in the great scheme of things and did not demand to be treated as intellectual equals-even if they were. North American women, particularly Canadian women - the ones he had met at university - seemed to him to assume that they were on equal footing in all matters. He was uncomfortable with the notion that there could be two acknowledged heads of any household. Even if it was the case, Scottish women knew to defer to their husbands in social settings. Anyway, he wasn't sure how to set things right between himself and Helen, or even if that was possible. It seemed that whenever she was around and he opened his mouth to speak, he either hurt Sarah's feelings or made Helen mad. So, he'd decided to steer clear as much as decently possible under the circumstances.

Matt glanced at his brother and noticed how closely he had been watching them, and how wistful and lonely Ian seemed. *Poor man; he does look done in.* Instinctively, he got up from his chair and moved over to sit beside Ian.

"You're looking tired brother – are those students keeping you busy? Sarah tells me you have a particularly heavy course load."

"It is heavy – or maybe I'm just feeling my age," replied Ian, feeling glad his brother was there since Sarah was fully ensconced in a conversation with Helen. "Nolan MacDermott is off on stress leave for a couple of months and I've picked up one of his classes. I was supposed to have had a lighter load this term so I could do some research, but there wasn't anyone available to pick up Nolan's course in mid-stream." Because he had several terms of full course loading with no time for research, the faculty had promised to drop two courses this term so he could work on an article he'd had in mind for some time. Then Nolan had had what used to be called a nervous breakdown – was off on stress leave, and his courses had to be parceled out to his colleagues. Ian was glad to help out. He and Nolan had worked together for seven years and co-authored a couple of articles. But the additional course meant that his plans for more time with Sarah and the children, and on his research, were diminished. He had hoped to have more time to spend with his family – sometimes he felt like a stranger to them, although the boys seemed to take it in stride that daddy either had to work late or close himself up in the study every night for a few hours. He knew Sarah needed a break in the evenings, and he tried to do his best to take the children as soon as he got home until dinner, and as much as possible at the weekend. But he knew it wasn't enough – for Sarah or for himself. He wanted to spend more time with the boys and he had barely a chance to get to know his baby girl.

"I'm sorry to hear about Nolan – I hope he pulls out of it soon" said Matt. "I heard he and his wife split up – that can't help the situation."

"No" agreed Ian. "It didn't. It seems to be happening a lot these days." At the back of Ian's mind was a worry that if he somehow didn't sort out his workload, he too could face something like that down the road. The thought was unbearable to him because he loved Sarah and the children so deeply and could not imagine them separated from each other. When she had taken the children to visit her parents in Canada over the years, Ian had been so lonely. He hadn't let on how lonely because he had wanted her to enjoy her stay and not worry about him. He had delved into his research during those times, and perhaps a bit too much whisky as well, although he gave the latter up when they returned.

"I was wondering if there is anything I can do to help. Sarah looks tired too. I know I wasn't much use when there was so much to do about the estate business, but I would like to make it up to you somehow." Matt looked down at his glass as he said this. He had felt Ian's resentment over his serial disappearances whenever there were family matters that had to be attended to. Ian had never said anything about it to him, but Matt sensed his disapproval.

Ian was surprised by the offer. He had resigned himself to Matt's lack of responsibility where the estate matters were concerned. On some level, he admired Matt's devil-may-care attitude and ability to drop everything to follow his whims. Generally, though, Ian knew that he facilitated Matt's lack of family responsibility – partly because of his impatience to attend to things and get them done as soon as possible. He wasn't going to waste time waiting for Matt to help out. And also because he didn't want to be the heavy-handed older brother. He didn't want to do anything to alienate Matt because he wanted Matt in his childrens' lives, and he was just fun to be around – when he was around.

"Thanks Matt – it's a nice offer. We may just take you up on it. Are you sure you are up to spending more time around us. It's not terribly exciting compared to your life."

"I've had enough excitement for awhile. A bit too much of spending time with shallow people who don't really give a damn about me. Don't get me wrong, I have had a few years of hedonistic pleasure as a result of the attention and money I've made with my painting. I had no idea my self-indulgent musings with brushes and paint would be perceived as art, let alone wanted by anyone. It was as much of a surprise to me as I am sure it was to you. Contrary to appearances, I am just as deeply rooted in our family as you are Ian. I know this will come as a shock, but what I want more than anything else right now is to be an uncle to my nephews and niece. When you and Sarah asked me to be Helen's godfather, I was so grateful – I am grateful and proud. It means a lot to me, and it made me really think about my life and where I was going with it. I want to be a positive influence and an important person in little Helen's life – and the boys." Matt paused. He hadn't meant to spill his guts like this. Ian listened to his brother intently, noticing how vulnerable Matt looked. He knew Matt loved the boys, and they him, but he was away quite a bit and had never seemed overly interested in their family life. Matt's little speech was a revelation to Ian who had always perceived him to be completely self-centred. He wasn't sure how to respond to it. He didn't have to, as Sarah's attention had switched to them at that moment.

"Matt. You must ask Helen about the dream she had last night. It was quite frightful for her."

"Yes," ventured Ian, "I'd like to hear about it too. We thought something was really wrong when we heard her cry out in the middle of the night." Ian had meant to sound pleasant and friendly, but he could see from the way Helen glared at him, he hadn't come across that way – at least not to her.

"I'm afraid I woke Ian and Sarah in the wee hours," Helen said somewhat crisply. "It was a terrible dream I have no idea where it came from." She told them about the child's hand gripping her own, and its manifestation from the hearth of the fireplace in her room.

"That is an odd one." ventured Matt, looking concerned but smiling at the same time. "Do you think it has anything to do with you becoming a godmother, Helen? I know it caused me to do some soul searching of my own. In fact, I was just telling Ian about it."

"No. I'm quite sure it has nothing to do with me being a godmother," said Helen, looking somewhat annoyed. *He barely knows me – how dare he make this kind of association as if I am afraid of being a godmother.* "It was very intense, and it felt like I was being pulled into someone else's life or struggle or–I don't know how to describe it. It had nothing to do with me but everything to do with that little person. It was so real – it sent shivers right through me."

"Certainly a bad dream, that's for sure," Ian said as if to conclude the discussion. "Well, if you will excuse me, I think I will head to bed for some dreams of my own – hopefully undisturbed." He winked at Helen as he said this, but it provoked another glare from her.

"I'll do my best to keep quiet tonight, Ian," she shot back, "I certainly don't want to disrupt your beauty sleep again."

"I am just teasing you a bit Helen – don't take it so seriously. Come Sarah, let's leave Matt and Helen to explore the meaning of her celestial adventures. The baby will be awake for her feeding soon and you need to rest." Ian took Sarah's hand and helped her out of her chair.

"Yes, that's true. Goodnight you two. Help yourselves to everything. See you in the morning." Sarah yawned, and left the room with Ian.

"Is it my imagination or do you not particularly like my brother?" asked Matt as he tended to the fire.

"Remarkably, I haven't really spent that much time with him, Matt, even though we met in college and he's been married to my best friend for eight years. I'm sure he's a fine person; he must be if Sarah loves him. He and Sarah have certainly produced beautiful children together." Helen hoped he wouldn't pursue her view of Ian. She was really trying to be tolerant and respectful of Sarah's life and everyone in it so that the visit would go as smoothly as possible. Matt noticed that as Helen changed the subject she positioned a few cushions around herself, creating a soft barrier between him and herself.

"Indeed they have, and I intend to spend as much time with them as possible. I haven't been around a lot, but, fortunately for me, the boys seem to like me in spite of that."

"I understand what you're saying, Matt, because I've wished I could be closer and see them more often myself. Probably more for me than for them." Helen laughed, "I don't know if Ian could tolerate me for more than a couple of weeks every ten years!" Matt chuckled and nodded his head.

"Actually, Helen, Ian really admires you. He told me about you when he returned with Helen from Canada. He said you were incredibly devoted to your studies. That is one thing I absolutely know about Ian – he is impressed by people who have a focus and purpose in life and are devoted to them." Matt sounded a bit resentful. "Believe me, I know from having reaped his wrath from the opposite perception of me. Not that he often says anything to me, he wouldn't, but I can tell from the way he looks at me sometimes that he thinks I'm a n'er-do-well." Matt switched gears. "But we were talking about you, weren't we? He tells me now that your current research is advancing the treatment of breast cancer. Did you know our mother died of breast cancer when we were quite young?" Helen was stunned. Sarah had never mentioned this to her.

"No, I didn't know. How terrible for you."

"I can hardly remember because I was very young, but Ian was nine and he was very sad for a long time – I do remember that. Our father more or less left it to the housekeeper to look after us, although he was very particular about our education – especially Ian's – I was just kind of a spoiled scamp and left to do as I pleased most of the time. Ian had to study a lot – there were high expectations of him. And, believe me, you did not want to disappoint my father."

Helen wondered why Sarah had never mentioned any of this to her, especially since Helen's own mother had surgery to remove breast cancer five years ago, and had been in remission since then. Perhaps that was the reason Sarah hadn't said anything. She knew how anxious Helen was about her mother's situation, and how helpless and completely useless she felt at the time, despite being a doctor and expert in breast cancer research. Since then, Helen was on a mission to find a better method of early diagnosis and a means of determining genetic probability and preventative treatment. Helen realized that she had been very intent on the events of her own life, and really hadn't taken an interest in anything or anyone for some time. She made up her mind to ask Sarah about all of this the next day. The fire had died down again, and both Helen and Matt were half asleep on the generous cushions of their respective sofas.

"I think I will turn in now. I'm still a bit jet-lagged and, as you now know, I didn't sleep all that well last night."

"Aye. I'm ready as well. Before you go up, what are your plans for tomorrow? Is there anything I can help with for the party?" Matt asked, leaning forward to close the glass doors on the fireplace.

"Sarah mentioned that we have an appointment around two o'clock to see the reverend. Apparently she wanted to meet me before the baptism. I guess you know her already." Helen replied.

"Oh yes. I know Reverend McDougall. She was the first woman to be ordained in our area. And, of course, she is the pastor at our family church. I usually see her at Christmas and Easter. She is very nice but rather inquisitive. At least I have found her to be so. She certainly takes an interest in the families of her congregation."

"Well, as far as I know, that is our main errand for tomorrow. Most everything else has been arranged for Sunday. Will you be staying until then?"

"No, but I thought I could stay and look after the baby and the boys when they get home from school, if you and Sarah wanted some time together. I would also like to take you to do a bit of sight-seeing next week. You should see our castles. They are all over the place, but there are a few that you must go through."

"Thank you, Matt. For both offers. You are very kind." Helen appreciated the offer of going around to see a bit of Scotland; however, she was not really interested in castles. But this was clearly important to Matt, so she did not want to offend him by declining.

Chapter 4 – New Acquaintances

The next morning, as Helen stood outside admiring the view of the rear garden and sipping her coffee in the cool, fresh air, she thought about her first two days in Scotland. An uninterrupted sleep had refreshed her, and she felt quite relaxed and ready for the day's activities. Sarah and Matt were busy rearranging the dining and sitting rooms to accommodate Sunday's guests. The housekeeper's arrival was imminent, and Sarah and Helen planned to leave for an early lunch in town before their appointment with Reverend McDougall. Matt was staying home with the baby, and would be there to greet the boys and give them their tea when they returned home from school. Helen looked forward to some time alone with Sarah. They had been so busy with arrangements for the baptism that they had not really had a good catch-up as yet. Helen was anxious to ask Sarah about Ian's mother – and why she had never mentioned this before.

Actually, there were several subjects on which she would seek both explanation and advice from Sarah. Sarah had just begun her dissertation for her PhD when she and Ian decided to get married and move to Scotland. She had been doing research into genetic testing for cancer risk and the potential for early preventative treatments – one aspect of her doctoral study- and Helen wanted her views on its application to breast cancer. Presently, in terms of technological support for breast cancer diagnosis, they continued mainly to rely on mammograms – which seemed an archaic method in Helen's estimation, but she felt she did not have the expertise necessary to challenge it as the best diagnostic tool. After all, it did work a reasonable percentage of the time. However, that hardly consoled those who had cancer that was not detected through mammograms. Her own mother's cancer had been missed in its early stages; however, and Helen felt very strongly that the technology experts need to be pushed to come up with a more effective and accurate solution. She often thought, and sometimes expressed, that if the experts, who were predominantly male, had to have mammograms, the equivalent being having their testicles crushed between two steel plates, there would already be an alternative and effective diagnostic tool for breast cancer. However cynical it sounded, she believed that some element of it was true, although prostrate exams were no picnic either – but hardly comparable to the pain and diagnostic vulnerability of the mammogram. More recently, there had been advances in genetic testing for women whose mothers had survived or perished as a result of breast cancer. Some who tested positive for certain virulent types of cancer were opting to have radical mastectomies of both breasts as a preventative measure. Helen was focused on finding less drastic preventative measures for those at greater risk of developing cancer. She knew that Sarah had made some intriguing findings during her research projects, and was hopeful that they have an opportunity to discuss them.

"Oh there you are!" exclaimed Sarah. " I was looking through the house for you. I'm ready to go. Matt and I are finished, and Betty is here – I've given her instructions – let's go Lenny, before Matt realizes what he's gotten himself into!" Sarah continued to chatter away, and Helen thought that she seemed a bit like her old self today. She felt a pang as she looked at her friend's animated features. Sarah was always looking after everyone; she had always been like that. Helen suddenly realized how much Sarah had watched over her as they were growing up, making sure Helen was included in games or invitations to parties when she knew that Helen was not a popular choice amongst their classmates throughout their school and university days. She had often wondered why she had been invited to parties because she knew the other kids didn't really feel comfortable around her. Hell, she wasn't really comfortable with herself, so how could others be? Except for Sarah. Sarah treated her as a close friend, and as a sister really – Helen felt most normal when she was around Sarah because Sarah accepted her for just as she was.

As they drove into Aberdeen, Helen admired the granite buildings and the pretty streets. It was a beautiful, clear day and the granite glinted and sparkled in the sun. Some complained that Aberdeen was a dull, grey looking place, and Helen could not understand this view when all around her the stately structures shone and sparkled as if embedded with crystals. Granted, there were many cloudy days in the Scottish north and under those circumstances, perhaps there was a dulling effect. Helen failed to see how it could be described as dreary though, as some had described Aberdeen when they heard that was where she was going. She loved the architecture of the place, and it appeared to be a clean and well-kept city. As they had a bit of time, Sarah drove her to the University of Aberdeen campus and they walked around the green bowls of meticulously mown grass between the ancient stone buildings.

"I love to come here from time to time, just to be in the environment, "sighed Sarah, obviously happy to be there. "Sometimes I go to the library to stand between the stacks and smell the books. I love that smell, and I miss it. You know what I mean, Lenny. When I say that to Ian – he laughs – but I know you feel the same way."

"Yes, I do. It's one of my favourite places to be when I need to think about something." Helen sat down on a bench and took in the peaceful beauty of the surroundings. "But I think there are only a few of us who feel that way – a lot of people hate being in the library. Especially now with so many developing allergies to everything. Mind you, I think the majority of people are simply allergic to books. It seems as if the library is a lot emptier than it used to be. Maybe it's just me getting older. Remember how we used to have to stake out our spots in the library, and then take staggered breaks so one of us could protect the other's territory? Now the desks are mostly empty. I guess a lot are doing their research on the Internet."

"You know, Ian says the same thing. He says the quality of the papers he gets is not as good in some respects and maybe that's why. Not enough of toughing out going through hundreds of books to support your argument. There is also a tremendous problem now with plagiarism – but that's a discussion you can have with Ian. You should hear him go on about it. I only hope the boys don't get spoiled by the Internet. I have to say, for a couple of academics and avid readers, our kids are not interested in reading for entertainment. It's hard for us to accept." Sarah, who had been relaxing on the bench, jumped up suddenly and looked at her watch. "Oh, god, Lenny, we'd better get going if we want to have lunch and be on time to meet Reverend McDougall. She is very punctual, and doesn't like it when people are late. I know this from experience."

They had lunch in one of the small, modern bistros that had been opening in Aberdeen recently. It was sparsely decorated but clean and comfortable, and it was busy with university students having a pint with their soups. It was Friday, and everyone seemed to be in good spirits with the impending weekend. Sarah and Helen ordered bowls of the house soup, served with generous portions of crusty rye bread and slices of gouda. Helen always liked to order soup when she traveled because she thought that wherever you were, people generally made good soup. Also, because a certain amout of boiling was involved, it was less likely one would become ill as a result of eating it. So far, this had been a good hunch, and no less so on this day. She talked Sarah into a glass of a full-bodied Shiraz to accompany the soup, and chatted contentedly throughout the meal. They followed up with the day's special dessert which happened to be sticky-toffee-pudding – apparently a Friday staple at this bistro, and a popular one. It was delicious; it had just the right texture and the sauce was divine. A good cup of tea brought them to their senses again, and they left with minutes to spare to make their appointment with the Reverend.

She was waiting for them on the step at the side door that led to her office. It was a magnificent church, or Kirk, not the largest in Aberdeenshire, but one of the oldest. The Wallaces' family home, where Ian and Sarah lived, was only a short distance down the country road from the church. Ian and Sarah had a second wedding here when they arrived from Canada newly married. Ian's family insisted at the time and they obliged. There was no question that all the children should receive a special blessing in the church, despite having already been baptized in Toronto. Though Ian and Sarah were not overly involved in the church, other than to show up for most Sunday services, they did provide consistent financial support, as was stipulated by the elder Wallace's will after his death. He hadn't been a strict religious man; however, he valued the role of the church in society and believed in the universality of its sanctuary for its members. He would always say that no matter where you were in the world, if you found your church, you would be at home. Ian and Sarah had decided to continue with the family tradition. Once the children were older, they could determine for themselves to what extent they would exercise their religions beliefs. Sarah believed that a person did not need a church to experience spirituality, but she accepted that the Wallaces closely associated with their Anglican church, if not for their own religious convictions, out of respect for their parents and the significance of traditon.

"We're not late are we?" worried Sarah as they came up the walk. "The appointment is for two o'clock, Reverend?"

"Aye, it is, Mrs. Wallace, "smiled the Reverend. "I just stepped out to get some air. It's such a bonny day. And this must be Miss Brooks, it's lovely to meet you. Come in." The Reverend led the way into the cool, dark hall. She was a tiny, if slightly stocky woman with black hair and eyes. Her voice was strong and clear and there was an authority about the way she walked and gestured. "Here we are." She opened the door to a lovely room with stone walls and floor, a fireplace and beautiful stained glass, leaded windows. The furniture was heavy and carved and she seemed somewhat dwarfed when she sat behind an immense desk that was laden with stacks of papers and books.

"Well, Miss Brooks. You're to be the baby's godmother. It's a blessing to be a godmother you know?" Reverend McDougall looked closely at Helen as she nodded in agreement. "There really is no greater privilege than being a godparent, other than creating life oneself. With the help of God, and the holy spirit, of course. Are you aware of the significance of the responsibility, dear?" Before Helen could respond, she went on. "You are responsible for the child's spiritual guidance and well-being – for her entire life. Naturally you will share that responsibility with the godfather, Mr. Matthew Wallace. Baptism is sacred and must be done with thought, resolution and conviction."

Helen was rather startled by the intensity of the woman, but indicated with a nod that she understood. "I assure you that I accept that responsibility Reverend McDougall. I would not have agreed to it if I had any doubts about my ability to fulfill my role. I did some research at home into what was involved and I am comfortable with the expectations."

"I'm pleased to hear it, Miss Brooks. Forgive me if I seem blunt, but I find that many are not. They show up for the cake and champagne, and then disappear until the weddings of their godchildren years later! Were you baptized Miss Brooks?"

"Yes I was baptized in the Anglican church," said Helen, startled again by the question. "Why?"

"It's tradition here, you might say. It's thought that those who have been baptized with holy water are more likely to appreciate the importance. Although there is no empirical evidence to back that up. I know you are a scientist Miss Brooks, or should I be calling you Dr. Brooks?"

"Actually, you may call me Helen, please," smiled Helen. "Let me just say that I am honoured and humbled by Sarah and Ian's request to be little Helen's godmother. I am thrilled in fact. Sarah and I are like family, and I absolutely promise to be there for her children, spiritually and otherwise."

"That's fine, Helen. That's all I need to hear." The Reverend stood up and came around her desk and took Helen's hand. "The Wallaces have been a part of this church for generations, and I am very pleased to be a part of this generation's experience. I must say good afternoon now, as I have another meeting now about a wedding. Thank you both for coming, and I will see you on Sunday."

"Thank you, Reverend," murmured Sarah, as she and Helen left the office and walked past a young, frightened looking couple who clearly were intimidated by the Reverend. As they left they overheard her as she ushered them, red-faced, into her office, "So you want to get married. It's a serious business and not to be taken lightly. It's more than just a sanction for a romp in the bedroom, laddy, do you understand? It's a great responsibility." Sarah and Helen burst out laughing as they left the churchyard.

"She is a character, isn't she? I told you." Sarah looked at Helen wondering what she was thinking. "I hope she hasn't put you off Lenny. Thank you for being so great with her; she really means well and looks out for our family."

"I think she's great, Sarah. And we have that in common. I agree with what she said, even though I'm not an actively religious person. I do have my beliefs, Sarah, and I'm fine with the role of godmother, really. I am only concerned that I may not live up to her standards, being so far away, but I will do my best."

"I know you will, Lenny. It was important to us to have the children baptized, but not necessarily for the religions reasons one might usually expect. I don't know, for me it's seems as if it gives them some kind of special protection for life. I like to believe that in addition to what their mother and father can do to protect them from the world's evils and disappointments, there is some kind of special layer of protection that comes from having that connection with something in the spiritual realm."

"I understand that – I believe I would do the same if I had children. I know that's what my parents may have been thinking when they had me baptized – maybe yours too. After all, neither of our parents were really avid church goers, were they? I mean, of course we went for Easter, Christmas, Mother's and Father's days, and Palm Sunday's.

Not that much in between those though. I remember that after a few years of Sunday school I determined my own spiritual path and it didn't really involve being in a church every Sunday. But I don't think that makes me any less spiritual, do you?" Helen looked at Sarah with her characteristic intensity.

Sarah smiled. "Frankly, I think it makes you more spiritual. But don't tell Reverend McDougall I said that – she would disagree. She has been tirelessly trying to convince us to be more involved in the church. I think she thinks we should be given the Wallaces' history of support and active participation. I actually went to some of the ladies's teas, and Ian has gone to what they call the men's club – it's actually a bible discussion group. Neither of us pursued these activities because we feel rather uncomfortable in them – as if we're kind of frauds. These people, for the most part, are very sincere about their religious beliefs, and Ian and I are just not of that mindset."

"That's exactly it, Sarah. I know what you mean. I always felt like an outsider and that there was something wrong with me because I just couldn't believe in the interpretation of the bible, and how it could influence people to behave in that churchy way. I actually found it nauseating, and, to me, it seemed that many of them were too sanctimonious. If you didn't seem enthusiastic about what they were saying, there was some sort of unspoken disapproval. Although, I have to admit, it was some of the women from our church – you know – the one my parents still go to once in awhile, who called as soon as they heard mom had cancer. They brought over meals and took her to appointments when I couldn't get there on time. There is something very special about the support you can tap into at a church. Don't get me wrong; my parents have gone there for years – when they've gone. Anyway, I really appreciated their support, and it came without any "preaching". I was impressed. By the way, Sarah, while we're sort of on the topic, why didn't you ever tell me that Ian's mother died from breast cancer?" Sarah looked surprised. They were at the car and they got in, but Sarah paused after she put the key into the ignition.

"Oh. Did Matt tell you?" she asked. When Helen nodded, she went on, "There are a couple of reasons, Lenny. I didn't know myself until I told Ian about your mother's cancer. That's when he told me about it. I don't know why he never mentioned the particulars of her death before, and, dope that I can be sometimes, I just never asked how she died. Also, I was more focused on you and your mother at the time, and I didn't want to really talk about someone else's experience to you, especially since she did die from it. I thought it might make you even more upset. I guess too, I mean it was so long ago, before they had the treatments they do now, but it just didn't seem appropriate to bring it up." Helen recognized, once again, Sarah's protectiveness of her feelings. She was very sensitive to what made Helen anxious, uncomfortable and unhappy.

"Thank you, Sari. You're always looking out for me – even with three kids of your own. What would I do without you? That's a rhetorical question by the way." Sarah laughed at her. "I wondered why you hadn't mentioned it to me, but, you know, I figured it was for my sake for some reason."

"It was at the time, and, then – well, I just forgot about it again." Sarah started the car and they began the short drive home. "How is your mom these days, Lenny? Any reoccurrences?"

"No, thank god. She's fine. She has regular checks every four months just to be sure. I'd like her to have an MRI every six months just to be on the safe side, but she says there are too many others waiting in line with cancer who need the appointments more than she does – you know what she's like." Helen sighed. She had been arguing with her mother about this for a couple of years now. It was not a usual course of action for cancer patients to use MRI as a preventative measure, and her mother was right – there were year-long waiting lists for diagnosis. Mind you, if it was thought that the patient had a malignant tumour-they were given priority and usually did not have to wait. It came down, sometimes, to degrees of malignancy – and that is where Helen had difficulty. She could not understand why the funding was not there to support an adequate number of machines for dealing with all critically ill people. In Helen's estimation, it came down to politics, and it enraged her that people's lives, along with the lives of their families, were held at ransom because of political posturing and grandstanding. "Sari, I want to talk to you a bit about your research. I really think that genetic predisposition to breast cancer and early prevention treatments are the key to better diagnosis and effective interventions."

"Oh god, Lenny. It's been years since I've looked at that stuff. Mind you, I do still get the journals because, technically, I am still considered part of the program – on a leave of absence. My time is running out though; if I am going to finish my dissertation, I have to do it within the next two years. But at least I have been able to keep up, to some extent, on progress in diagnostic technology, and some of the issues." Sarah frowned as she thought about some of things she'd been reading. "You know, from what I gather, the debate about using genetic testing for preventative treatment or diagnosis of breast cancer has been going on for quite some time now, as you know, and I agree that some of the reasons for not doing it do seem to be more about politics than anything else." As they turned into the driveway, they could see Matt out in the garden with the boys and the baby. "I'll tell you what, Lenny. Next week when you're out sightseeing with Matt, I'll go through some of my files to see what I can dig out for us to discuss. Actually, it will be good for me to do that anyway. I really must think seriously about whether or not I am going to get that damn thesis written." Sarah's eyes lit up as she talked about delving into her boxes of files and going through her work and the articles she had collected and put away over the years.

"Thanks, Sari. I know you have enough to do without that, but I would appreciate it." *Now this is more like the Sari I know. Look how excited she is about her work. If she can find the time, this may help her get back on track with her thesis and finish.* Helen did not want to add to Sarah's endless list of tasks, but she did think too that Sarah could use some intellectual diversion, and she did seem enthusiastic about looking through her boxes. As they walked from the car to the garden, Helen saw Ian peering out of the house from behind the curtain in his study. *He's home early–I wonder why.* Matt greeted them enthusiastically and handed over the baby to Sarah. The boys jumped around their mother and Helen, obviously glad to see them come home.

"We're all happy to see you two," laughed Matt, "I'm but a poor substitute for their mother! Right boys? Yes – did I hear you say 'yes'? All right – now you're in for it – just wait until I catch you!" The boys gleefully ran off and split up – each going a different direction down one of the garden paths, while their uncle chased them, waving his arms like a madman. Sarah and Helen chuckled, and even Ian laughed as he greeted them at the door.

"I offered to take them over, ladies, but Matty wouldn't hear of it. I don't know where he gets all the energy to be able to keep up with them. I've managed to get my papers marked, so I'm free for the evening. Want some help with dinner, Sarah?" Ian followed them into the kitchen and took the baby from her mother.

"Thanks sweetheart, but I think Betty was going to leave a stew in the oven…yes- here it is and it looks yummy. I bought some nice bread at the bakery and we'll keep it simple tonight." Sarah was pleased that Ian had made the offer. Helen was surprised and a bit suspicious.

"Well in that case, I think I will take little Helen out to watch her brothers and uncle run amok in the garden." Ian walked outside with the baby and began talking to her and pointing out the various flowers and trees to her, interspersed with a few shouts of encouragement to his sons who were easily evading the clutches of their fatigued uncle.

They all came in later and sat down to a hearty dinner in the kitchen. The evenings were chilly, but the kitchen was warm and cozy. Everyone was hungry and enjoyed the simple, but delicious fare. Helen tidied the kitchen while Sarah got the children to finish their homework and get ready for bed. Ian and Matt had gone to the study and were having a good discussion about something - Helen could not quite make out what-but heard them laugh once in awhile. She felt at home, and peaceful – more at ease than she had been in some time. Matt decided to stay over again that night and the next to help the next day with any last minute details for Sunday's activities. Sarah seemed more relaxed too, and even Ian was enjoying himself with his brother around. Helen felt calm, but really tired that night, excused herself early to go to bed, and fell into a sound sleep as soon as her head hit the pillow.

Chapter 5 - The Baptism

Sunday dawned clear and sunny; a perfect day. Helen laid in bed and looked out her window. She felt at home. It was nice. She was looking forward to the day's events and was excited and a bit nervous at the same time. They had all spent Saturday doing the last minute preparations and decorating the house with flowers. Even the boys had helped; they seemed excited about Sunday's event.

Helen was not particularly comfortable around people at the best of times, with the exception of family and very close friends. She was extremely uncomfortable around strangers and knew that she did not communicate particularly well with people she did not know. Helen decided to muster everything she had to be sociable today. She really wanted the day to be perfect for Sarah, and for them to be confident that she had been the right choice for godmother. Also, Matt was so charming and affable – she was sure everyone probably loved him, and she did not want the contrast between them to be too striking.

A gentle knock at her door roused her from her sleepy musings. She sat up against the pillows and smiled.

"Come in."

"Good morning Lenny. Oh I am so glad you are awake. Isn't it a glorious day? I am so happy you are here." Sarah sat down beside her and sighed contentedly. "I was just in the dining room and everything looks so lovely. The flowers are amazing and you have decorated the rooms so beautifully. Thank you, sweetie."

"No – thank you, Sari. I love being here with you and the children. And I think Matt is really nice. Really, they all pitched-in to help." Helen stopped short of saying anything about Ian. She was pleased with the way everything was going, and especially that Sarah seemed so relaxed and more like herself the past couple of days. Her initial trepidations about Matt had disappeared as she got to know him, and because he seemed so different from Ian. She could also see that Ian was perhaps trying to be less obnoxious to her than usual, and she was surprised that he had actually spoken about her research to anyone. Maybe it was possible for old dogs to learn new tricks, she thought to herself, but she was going to keep a close eye on Mr. Ian just the same. Her concern was Sarah's welfare and she really wanted to see Sarah conduct herself with more confidence – more like she used to be. Although, Helen had to admit, it was clear Sarah loved her role as mother and wife (in Helen's mind it had to be in that order). Helen, once again, wished they lived closer together so she could help Sarah with the children and to keep Ian on his toes as much as possible.

"Let me get myself ready, and then I will help you with the children." Helen suggested. "I think Matty said he was going to help Betty with breakfast and to clear up, as she wants to come to church too."

"Yes. In fact they are in the kitchen now. It's so great to have him here too. Anyway, that sounds perfect. I'll get dressed and ready too, and then we can get the boys up. Ian has baby in bed with him right now, so I'm clear to focus on myself. Hopefully I can get myself looking presentable by the time the baby wakes up! I need a lot more time than I used to – that's for sure   See you in about an hour." she said, laughing as she left Helen's room and closed the door.

Helen tidied her room and laid out her clothes on the bed. She had brought a pale, shimmery grey-green suit to wear for the baptism. It was an Italian-made pantsuit made of stretch cotton sateen, and it draped beautifully on her slim figure. The colour enhanced the green of her eyes, and she had some simple crystal jewelery to wear with it. She didn't usually spend much time shopping; there was never time for much but work. For this important occasion, however, she wanted something special. She had gone straight to Holt Renfrew for her ensemble – shoes to earrings. One-stop shopping was her forte when she had to do it, and she had spent four focused hours there getting everything she needed. It had been an expensive outing but her purchases were classics that would wear out before they went out of style. Given that she rarely went out, maybe to the odd fundraiser for research or the hospital, she would likely have her clothes forever.

She had also bought Sarah and little Helen the same necklace as the one she would wear today. She planned to give Sarah hers to wear today, and the baby would have one for when she was grown-up. They were high-end, Tiffany gold heart pendants encrusted with Swarovski crystals, and engraved on the back with the baby's birth date, and "God Bless Helen Sarah Wallace". She had also brought a beautiful little outfit for the baby to wear after they returned home from the church, and a Canada Saving's Bond. Helen had given the boys savings' bonds as well when they were born. Each was for five thousand dollars and her intent was that by the time the bonds matured, the children would have a nice little savings account to help get them started in their chosen pursuits.

She went down to the kitchen after she dressed, looking for a cup of coffee. Breakfast was prepared and laid out buffet style. Matt was not there, and Betty informed her that he had gone to get dressed. Sarah came looking for her soon after, and they went upstairs to get the boys and the baby ready. Sarah looked wonderful in a Chanel style lavender silk dress and jacket. She was thrilled with Helen's gift and immediately put the necklace around her neck.

"Oh, thank you, Helen – it's gorgeous! You know how I love crystals." Sarah admired herself in the mirror in the baby's room. Little Helen was wearing the lace gown that her father, uncle and brothers had all worn for their baptisms and christenings. It was beautiful Irish lace over a heavy but fine cotton dress. There was an antique cast to the white colour of the dress, and the lace had glints of gold thread throughout. The baby was such a little doll with those round blue eyes and red lips. She had a gold lace bonnet over her glossy curls and little gold lace booties.

"What a little princess you are baby!" exclaimed Ian as he picked her up and held her high in the air. He looked neat and handsome himself, in a dark suit and gold tie. "Sarah, you look amazing – so beautiful, dear. And, Helen, you look fantastic too – I almost didn't recognize you – you both look so glamorous." Ian felt sure they would appreciate his comments. Sarah looked wonderful, and he hadn't wanted to leave Helen out so he paid her a compliment too. Sarah smiled at him, and Helen raised one of her eyebrows as she thanked him, rather curtly. He then wasn't sure if he should have commented on her looks or not as she didn't appear to be too happy with his remarks. He was relieved when Matt and the boys came into the room.

"Well, are we all ready? My, what a stellar looking family we are! You too Helen – you are part of the family," commented Matt. "We'd best be off or we'll be late, and I don't think Reverend McDougall would be happy about that – do you?" With that, he expertly herded them all out of the house and into the two cars. They drove the short distance to the church and arrived as the last of the congregation was filing into the entrance. Reverend McDougall was standing outside next to the huge wooden doors, and she waved at them to come. They quickly climbed the stone steps and entered the church just ahead of the choir and the clergy who had been waiting in the hall to begin their procession to the front of the church.

The sermon was fairly brief that day, because of the baptism ceremony, but Reverend McDougall used her sermon as an opportunity to emphasize the importance of commitment and tradition, and the role of the church in the lives of its families. The baptism ceremony was lovely, and little Helen Sarah did not object in the least to having holy water poured over her head. As Helen stood beside Matt, listening to the words of the holy baptism, she suddenly felt a bit light-headed and there was a strange pressure on her shoulders. She looked around the church at the congregation, at the sunlight filtering through the coloured glass of the huge windows. As her eyes moved to the door of the church, she saw a woman standing in the shadows. Her face was very pale and she was wearing a shawl over her hair that draped down over a long dress. It appeared as if the woman was holding a small child, but she couldn't really tell. Helen wondered if the lady was late for the baptism ceremony, now underway, and afraid to come forward. She gave Matt a slight nudge, and when he leaned in she whispered in his ear, her concern for the poor woman, who would no doubt be in for a scolding from the Reverend. Matt looked toward the door as Helen refocused her attention on the ceremony.

"There is no one by the door, Helen," he whispered back to her discreetly. "She must have gone." Helen looked and the lady was not there any longer, nor was she seated in any of the pews. The pressure on her shoulders was gone too, and she felt a bit better, although she did feel sorry for the woman she had seen there, although she didn't know why the lady's circumstances or predicament, if she had one, should matter to her. *Not enough on your mind I guess,* she thought to herself.

Once the ceremony was over and the service ended, they took pictures on the steps in front of the church. Helen glanced around to see if there was any sign of the woman she had seen at the door, but she had obviously left. Helen felt a twinge of sadness for this stranger, and then forgot about her as Sarah and Ian began to introduce her to friends and cousins who had come for the baptism. After the group pictures were done, a procession of a dozen cars headed over to Ian and Sarah's house for the reception. Helen, Matt, Betty and the boys had left slightly earlier, leaving Ian, Sarah and the baby to pose for some last photos with the Reverend. They were to get the cake and sweets laid out in the dining room and open the champagne. Betty was running the show and they did exactly as she told them. There were little snacks of cheeses and crackers to be placed strategically around the sitting room and dining room, so that people could nibble and sip until the tea sandwiches, strawberries and cream were completely ready and set out in the dining room.

Helen told the boys to change into something more comfortable as they were pulling and scratching at their shirt collars and ties. Matt decided he'd had enough of his tie too and took it off. They went out to greet the guests as Helen and Betty loaded trays with glasses of champagne. She helped Betty pass out the glasses to the guests as they entered the house. She was glad to have something useful to do and it helped her to feel more comfortable as she greeted people and chatted while they took their glasses. It was such a lovely day that most wandered out into the garden and stood around or sat on the chairs and benches on the stone patio. The air was cool and fresh, but the sun was very warm as it beat down on the happy gathering. Jackets and wraps soon came off as everyone enjoyed the clear day.

    Sarah was relaxed and beaming with happiness. The baby had gone down for a nap and Matt was keeping an eye on the boys. Sarah and Ian were enjoying themselves immensely. She watched as Helen was moving around through the clusters of their friends and Ian's family, and she was quite impressed at how friendly and charming Helen could be. Sarah knew that this would be an effort for Helen and had expected that she might disappear to her room after a short time with so many people around. But Helen stayed until the last guest left at dusk, and then began helping Betty to clear away the dishes and remaining food from the table. Sarah was so grateful for Helen's presence and help; she had been so wonderful from the moment she arrived. Even Ian seemed to be enjoying her visit, although he was mostly thrilled to have his brother there with them for an extended period. When Ian was happy, there seemed to be such a better atmosphere in the house. Sarah often felt as if there was too much negative energy around them, and she attributed this to Ian's somewhat morose countenance and obsession with work. She knew he was frustrated at work and that this influenced his behaviour at home. It was such a relief and a pleasure to have him around when he was relaxed and enjoying himself. She decided that they would have to sit down and really talk about this seriously. She wanted her home environment to be positive and cheerful, especially for the children. She could see that the boys were so much happier when they knew their father wasn't shut up in his study or annoyed at something. They needed to see their father more often as he was this day. Sarah determined that there would be some efforts made to ensure that things did not go back to their usual pattern once Helen and Matt had gone. For the first time in a long time, she felt rested and just good about herself, and she wanted that to continue.

Matt decided to stay over one more night as he was tired from the day's activities and did not really want to drive the distance to Edinburgh. Helen was exhausted too, and by 10:30, they all decided it was time to go to bed. It had been a wonderful day – everyone said so – and everything had been as perfect as it could be.

Chapter 6 – Another Disturbance

Helen went up to her room feeling happier and more relaxed than she had felt in a long time. In spite of the fact that she had been busy from the moment of her arrival, she was experiencing a sense of belonging and peacefulness that she had never thought possible. It was an unusual sensation for her, and she was not sure what was causing this change within. Too tired to analyse the possible reasons for these new feelings, she got ready for bed and succumbed to sleep almost as soon as she laid her head on the pillow. She fell asleep thinking about how, now that the big event was over, she would have time to really visit with Sarah, and also to do some sightseeing. Matt was going to make a quick trip home to Edinburgh to see to some gallery business, and then he planned to return to take her on the promised tour of some area castles. She enjoyed his company and actually looked forward to more of it. She liked his sense of humour and lack of ego. He seemed genuine in his interest in getting to know her and showing her around a bit. Plus, he had, so far, accepted her as she was, and if he had any thoughts about her being socially awkward, he had kept them to himself. These were refreshingly pleasant experiences for Helen. It was nice for her to fall asleep lulled by images of such a lovely day, rather than the usual fretful worry and analysis over how she had been perceived by others.

Helen was in a deep sleep when she became aware of a chill down her back. It was so cold that she realized she was shivering. Instinctively she pulled the duvet closer around her neck so that no cold air could get under the blankets. As soon as she settled back into the pillow, on her way to resuming her sound sleep, the duvet was suddenly pulled from her shoulders as if someone had deliberately yanked at it. Through a haze of semi-consciousness, she again grabbed at the cover to bring it up again, but as she did so, she realized a tension in the blanket as though it was being pulled in the opposite direction. Thinking it must be caught on something, she turned to reach over the side of the bed to bring it up and encountered a shadowy image of a little pale hand grasping the other end of the duvet. A woman's voice whispered in her ear, "Help me! Help me….please help me." The tone was desperate and frightened. Startled awake, Helen sat bolt upright and wrenched the duvet completely onto the bed.

"Sari" she said quietly, "is that you?"

She sat there, now in a cold sweat, breathing heavily for several minutes, and looking around the dark room to see if there was anyone there. She could hear a child crying and wondered if the baby had awoken. The crying became fainter and more distant, and then stopped. Mustering up the courage to look over the side of the bed, she scanned the floor, the fireplace and the perimeter of the room. There was nothing. But she had felt in the pulling of the blanket, a life force that could not be denied. Was it a bad dream, she wondered, another bad dream – with the same little hand. Like the last time, it had seemed so real. She saw what she saw and she felt what she felt – how could this be a dream? Yet there was nothing in the room but moonlight coming in from the window. Why was this happening to her? She felt very cold and realized that she was shaking. She bundled herself in the blanket, wrapping it around her like a mummy, so that none of it was hanging off the sides of the bed. After a while, she felt warm again and drifted off. However, this time, suspended in that groggy state between sleep and wakefulness, she woke herself up every half hour until the sun came up. It was as if she was afraid to let herself go fully asleep again. Only after there was light in the room, did she finally drift back into deep slumber.

When Helen woke up it was mid-morning and she could hear the boys out in the garden playing. She felt kind of dull and heavy, and her head ached a little. *I am in need of a good cup of coffee.* She heaved herself out of the bed, went to the bathroom and splashed water on her face. She put on some jeans and a shirt, tidied the room and went downstairs to the kitchen. Sarah was there alone drinking coffee.

"Hi there you!" Sarah greeted her with a huge smile. "I am glad you were able to sleep in a bit, although with all the commotion, I was sure that we would wake you up." Sarah jumped up to get a cup and poured some coffee for Helen, who appeared to her to be somewhat disoriented. "Here you go sweetie. I made some Swedish pancakes this morning – just the way you like them, and there are lots of left over strawberries and cream to go with them." Sarah fussed over Helen as she would a child, setting a place at the table and bringing the food hot from the oven. There was bacon and ham too and some home-baked brown beans. All Helen's favourites, but which she never made for herself.

"Thank you, Sarah, you are my saviour – I desperately need some coffee and I can't believe you made the pancakes! Yum – I haven't had them for so long – what a treat." Helen sipped her hot coffee, savouring the flavour. Ian and Sarah banned anything but fresh coffee beans in their house, so every cup was freshly ground and delicious. She covered her pancakes with cream and strawberries and then poured maple syrup onto her plate so that it crept around the beans and bacon too.

"Where are Ian and Matt? And Baby? I heard the boys outside playing."

"Ian is in his study marking papers, and the baby is down for her morning nap. Matt left pretty early this morning, and said to say goodbye to you. We didn't want to wake you up. He also said he would be back late tomorrow so that you two could spend Wednesday and Thursday exploring a few castles in the area. That is if you are still interested." Sarah looked at Helen expectantly, hoping the response would be positive. She had hoped that Matt and Helen would get along well and find some common ground for a couple of reasons. Firstly, she was afraid that Helen would get bored spending another three weeks mired in their domestic activities, and, secondly, she secretly wished that there might be more than a friendship possible between two of her favourite people.

"Oh, I am sorry I missed seeing him off; I don't usually sleep so late. I had another dream I guess, more of a nightmare really, and I was awake for awhile. Of course I will be pleased to do some sightseeing. I have never thought much about exploring castles, but I guess that's what a lot of people do when they come to Scotland." Helen was glad to hear that Matt intended to come back. "It should be interesting really. I wonder if I can remember anything about Scottish history," she mused.

"Don't worry about that. Matt will give you a briefing on every place you go, I imagine," laughed Sarah. "He knows everything, and especially about the art and artifacts in each place. But, tell me, what kind of dream did you have? I hope it wasn't another bad one – I didn't hear you call out – mind you, I think we were all so tired that we slept like logs. What happened in this one?"

Helen told Sarah what had transpired and how real it all seemed, and how frightened she had felt when she woke up. They were both puzzled about what was causing Helen to have these types of dreams. It was so uncharacteristic of her to dream about anything. The last time she had had any semblance of a disturbing dream was when her mother was about to have her surgery. She had put that down to stress and to a feeling of complete helplessness to do anything for her mother, despite the fact that it was her own area of expertise. But that dream left her with a sense of frustration more than with fear. This was different. In these two dreams it was as if she was awake and caught in an experience that she could not escape, but, yet, she sensed that there was something expected of her – that she needed to do – she did not understand what it was.

"Well, I don't know what to say about it really, Lenny, but don't worry about it – I am sure it's some kind of weird product of everything that's been going on for the past week. Some way of getting rid of any stress you may have been under. You know that being around a lot of people for extended periods of time used to bother you. Is that still the case? Maybe it's just the result of all the hustle and bustle since you got here?" ventured Sarah, looking concerned and wanting to reassure Helen.

"Yes, you are probably right, and, yes, I am still like that. I do want to say, though, that while it may have been stressful for me, I haven't enjoyed myself so much for a long time. So if having a few bad dreams is what it takes to be able to have a good time in the company of others, then I am okay with it. It's just that dreaming anything of this sort is a new experience for me."

Helen finished her breakfast and refilled her coffee.

"So, what are we up to today Sari?" She was feeling more energetic and wanted to distract herself from the anxious feeling in her stomach. *Come on Helen, you don't want to waste any precious time with this nonsense. Besides, you don't want Ian to get wind of this, or he will make a big deal out of it.*

64

"Should we go outside with our coffee and watch the boys?" Sarah nodded, and out they went to sit in the mid-morning sun and enjoy the garden.

They spent the day around the house. Everyone was pretty tired, and the boys had been allowed to stay home from school for the day. Ian spent most of the time in his study working, which gave Helen and Sarah time to visit and reminisce about good times and old friends. Helen took the baby and held her and carried her about the entire day. She loved the little darling, who was really a miniature of her mother. The boys adored her too and didn't mind that their Aunty Lenny was so attentive to their sister. Of course Helen had time for them too, when the baby napped, and they read together in front of the fireplace.

It was peaceful, comfortable and pleasant to be in her best friend's home and life. But she could not rid herself of a nagging feeling in the pit of her stomach that something was wrong. It was annoying and disconcerting at the same time. She just wanted to relax and enjoy herself, but the experience of the night before was still vivid despite her efforts to push away the image of the little hand, and the voice begging for her help. It simply was not logical for her to be bothered like this, and she didn't like it. She determined that she must busy herself with activity. In her case, she decided, it was probably that she was not used to being so relaxed and needed to be doing more.

Chapter 7 – Sightseeing

As Matt drove back to his brother's home, he was preoccupied with the proposed castle tour for Helen. He decided, after some hours of musing, that he would first take her to three of his favourite castles in the Aberdeenshire area. Each was very different, not the least of which was the time period they were built. He felt these three provided an historic perspective on Scottish architecture within the general region during their respective times. He would then gauge Helen's reaction to these prior to planning more castle visits. There were so many possibilities, but, if she appeared to be interested, he planned to invite her to Edinburgh for a few days to see the historic landmarks in that area. Of course, Glamis Castle could be viewed on the way, if Helen had a desire to see the childhood home of the Queen Mother. It was his experience that some Canadians were interested and others were not.

Matt hoped that Helen would be interested because he liked her company, and because he was proud of his country's history, including the castles. While many Scots scorned the influx of tourists and their interest in exploring the country's castles, Matt had always been fascinated by these architectural treasures, and their stories and he loved to see the awe in the faces of tourists as they experienced these places for the first time. He also appreciated that tourism contributed immeasurably to the Scottish economy. He had benefited as well as he had sold many of his paintings to tourists. Maybe he should ask Sarah about his choices, and get her opinion on what she thought Helen might like to see. Matt felt that Helen was more comfortable with him than at first, and that they had gotten to know each other sufficiently well enough during the past week to manage a few days together. He also thought it might be good to provide Ian with a little breathing room in his house without visitors, so that he and Sarah could have some time to have their normal routine re-established after the business of the baptism preparations. It would be nice for Helen too, to get out beyond the immediate area. With the baby, the boys in school, and Ian working all the time, Matt surmised that sightseeing was too much for Sarah to manage, and that this was one way he could help out. He was very fond of his sister-in-law, and he had noticed that she had not been her usual bright self for some time. Helen's arrival had seemed to reenergize her to some degree, and he wanted to do what he could to contribute.

The castles he decided upon for Helen to see were Dunnottar, Drum and Crathes. All were fairly local, and he thought that he and Helen could manage the three in one day. They would go to Dunnottar Castle first. This was one of his favourite ancient places. It was just south of Aberdeen, along the eastern coastline, enroute to Edinburgh. Rising out of a steep cliff that overlooked the ocean, the ruins of the castle were breathtaking. The next stop would be Drum castle, which was in the countryside not far from the other side of the city. Home to the Irvine clan for generations, there were many interesting stories to tell, and, intact, it was possible to imagine the home's previous inhabitants and what life had been like there for them. They would visit their final destination, Crathes Castle, after a pub lunch. The entire interior of the castle was open to tourists, and the extensive, manicured gardens there were especially spectacular. He thought that Helen would love to spend the entire afternoon roaming the property. If the sun was out, and hopefully it would cooperate with his plans, walking around the Crathes gardens was a lovely way to spend an afternoon.

Matt arrived in time for dinner. He could see that Helen was pleased to see him and she seemed enthusiastic about his plans for them over the next couple of days. After dinner, Ian and Sarah tended to their children while Matt provided Helen with a brief history of each of the three castles they would visit the following day. Matt lit a fire in the cozy living room as Helen glanced through some brochures and information that Matt had brought with him.

"Would you care for a whisky, Helen?" asked Matt. "I am going to raid Ian's single malt collection."

"Sure – I'll join you. Thanks. No ice please – just neat. I seem to be developing a taste for it. Normally I would have a glass of wine or maybe a beer. But the flavour of some of these whiskyes! I never realized how good it was." mused Helen, rather astonished at herself for commenting on the merits of an alcoholic beverage. *What's with me? He'll think I'm a lush.* But she couldn't help herself and continued to chat. "Please call me Lenny, Matt. Helen sounds so formal. My family and friends call me 'Lenny'. They have ever since I can remember – after meeting Sarah-that is – she started it when we were three years old."

"Aye then, Lenny, I will. I hadn't wanted to presume, but thanks." He responded, smiling, and handed her a glass of whisky. "Cheers!" Matt was somewhat surprised, yet visibly pleased that Helen felt at ease enough with him to engage in a level of mundane chatter that was obviously not normally something she would do. He relaxed and sat down in Ian's chair by the fire. "If you like, we can go to one or two whisky tastings. Some of the most famous makers of single-malts are in the area you know."

"Cheers to you, Matt. That sounds like a nice idea; I would love it. And thank you for taking the time to show me around. I know you are busy and I appreciate it. I think too that it will be nice for Sari to have a little break too. Not that she has given me any indication that she wants one, but I think it will be good for all of them to have some time to themselves."

"It's my pleasure, Lenny. You are very thoughtful. It's apparent how close you are with Sarah." Matt continued, with a bit of a twinkle in his eye. "I hope you don't mind my saying, but I have noticed that it is a bit of an effort for you to tolerate my brother. I do know that he loves his family beyond anything and that things are just a bit trying for him at the university right now. So, don't worry about your friend, she will be fine. I plan to make more of an effort to help out as well. I am so grateful for Sarah and the children in my life, and especially for my brother. It's like we have a real family now. I don't know how much Sarah might have told you about us, but we were kind of lonely growing up. We responded to this in different ways, but now, what with being blessed with the company of my brother's family, I want to be more involved –at least as much as they want me to be." Matt paused to see if Helen looked interested or bored by his revelation. She was, however, leaning forward with her elbows on her knees, holding her drink with both hands. She was touched that Matt thought enough of her to share his personal thoughts.

"I think that's lovely, Matt. I am sure – no, I know that Sari loves to have you around anytime you can be here – she has told me so. And, if you don't mind my saying so, your brother is a nicer person when you are here. He seems more relaxed. Or maybe it's just that he feels outnumbered with me in the house." Helen smiled at the thought.

"You know, Lenny, Ian thinks very highly of you," Matt countered, feeling a bit defensive for his brother. "I suspect if he's been awkward that it is because he's always been a bit intimidated around you. You have to admit, you have accomplished a lot, published a lot, and, also, you are probably the most significant person to his wife outside of their little family."

The thought that she was intimidating to Ian had not occurred to Helen before Matt had mentioned it. She had always assumed that he was simply jealous of the close bond between her and Sarah. And also that their personalities simply just clashed. "As I said before, I am surprised to hear that my name or anything associated with me has ever come up in Ian's conversation," she responded candidly, putting her glass down on the table and leaning back into the pillows on the couch. "He was always so condescending with me, right from the beginning, and it really put me off. Normally I wouldn't have cared two hoots and put him in his place, but he was the love of my best friend's life, so I have always just put up with it. More or less. We have had our disagreements. Anyway, I have decided to be good on this trip. I do not want to in any way make life difficult for my Sari."

With that declaration, Helen looked a bit forlorn. He noticed that she seemed rather sad as she talked more about when she and Sarah and Ian were students, and what it had been like for her after her friend had left to live in another country. In the dimly lit room with the flicker of the flames lighting her pale face, there was an aura of vulnerability about her. Her white-blonde hair glinted in the light, and she seemed smaller than she was, as she curled her tall, slender frame into and behind the numerous cushions on the couch.

Matt thought she looked particularly lovely at the moment. There was no pretense about her, and she was so honest and candid when she spoke. This was so refreshing for him. Most of the women he knew were somewhat coy around him, and he always had the sense that they expected something from him. They were smart women, had good careers and were very capable. Yet, he hadn't ever come close to liking anyone enough to have a serious relationship, although he had dated a few women off and on for several months at a time. When it became clear to him that they had expected some kind of formal declaration of love or commitment, he had broken things off.

In his estimation, Helen was different. She was the same with everyone, he had observed, and was always thoughtful and intelligent in her conversation. He could see that she was clever in a way that could be intimidating, but he found her more intriguing than anything else and really enjoyed the discussions they had so far. He sensed that they had a 'meeting-of-the-minds', and found it easy to be around her. This had surprised him given his brother's description of what she was like.

Over a second glass of whisky, Matt and Helen agreed on their plan for the following day, and relaxed before the fire. They reminisced about the baptism and Helen entertained him with the details of her meeting with Reverend MacDougall. Matt described some of the towns that they would be driving through and suggested some possibilities for their lunch. As the fire died down, the two yawned and decided to get some sleep. Helen felt a bit of trepidation as she went upstairs. She was a bit worried that she might have another dream; however, she was tired and also excited about the next day's activities. She fell into a deep sleep almost immediately, no doubt aided in part by the consumption of the whisky. When she awoke, the sun was just coming up. She felt relieved, and rolled over to snatch another hour of sleep.

Matt was in the kitchen having breakfast with Sarah when Helen went downstairs. The boys were getting their bags ready for school, and Ian was just leaving for work.

"Good morning Helen," Ian ventured, "I hope you enjoy the sites today. Keep my brother in line though, lassie. He will talk your ear off with his history! I don't know what he finds so fascinating in those old castles, but if you're not careful, you'll be gone for days."

Matt looked a little crestfallen as these words were spoken. Helen noticed this and countered Ian's remarks immediately.

"I am in very capable hands with Matt. He is so knowledgeable and I am very excited to see whatever he has chosen to show me," offered Helen. "I am grateful that he has taken the time to do this for me. Your brother is a real gentleman, Ian."

Ian had also seen the disappointment in Matt's face, and realized that his attempt at humour had, once again, been lame. "I agree with you completely, Helen – on both counts. Have a good time and I will see you this evening." Ian kissed Sarah goodbye, and made a quick exit before anything else could be said. Helen looked a bit cross as she wondered if there was a double meaning in what Ian had just said. She tidied the kitchen while Sarah and Matt played with the baby. Matt had offered to drop the boys at their school on their way, so that they could have an extra hour at home to play and, for that, he was rewarded with enthusiastic hugs.

After they dropped the boys at their school, Matt and Helen set out for Dunnottar. It was a glorious day, a bit cool, but the sky was clear and blue, and the forecast was for an unusually warm afternoon. Helen gazed at the countryside as they drove, and found it to be incredibly beautiful. The rolling hills were a brilliant green and dotted with black and white sheep. It was so pastoral and peaceful. Helen felt happy. She marvelled at the kilometres of rough fencing, and at the pretty stone cottages and houses that they passed. Some of the houses looked like mini-castles with their turrets and old world architecture. She was really beginning to love this place. It almost felt like she had come home as she had an innate sense of belonging.

As they turned off of the main road to go to Dunnottar castle, Helen was struck by the view of the sea beyond the cliffs in the distance. As they got closer, she realized how ancient the site of the medieval castle was with its grey stone walls like a fortress along the edge of the cliffs. It was an incredibly steep drop from there to the waves below, and Matt warned her to keep an eye on where she was walking as they roamed around edges of the three acre site. Standing within the ancient walls and rubble of the castle itself, Helen felt an overwhelming sense of sadness and awe as Matt described the events that had transpired on that site. Particularly poignant were his stories of how prisoners of the castle were kept in one area and had been tortured and starved to death. Dunnottar was truly a magnificent setting that belied the tragedies that had played out there during the dark ages within its walls.

After a short drive to the countryside to the west of Aberdeen, they spent the rest of the morning going through Drum castle and grounds. Matt was such a wonderful guide that other tourists stopped to listen as he explained the history of various paintings, furnishings and objects in the castle. The National Trust guides and attendants paid attention too, and seemed impressed by his depth of knowledge about the family and events that had taken place there.

By noon, Helen was famished and agreed readily to Matt's suggestion that they stop for lunch. She actually felt a bit dizzy from the morning's sensory overload. Matt could see that she was looking a bit discombobulated and determined they needed a good break before heading to Crathes Castle. He decided to stop at the 'Falls of Feugh' in Banchory, which was close to their afternoon destination. It was a charming teahouse and restaurant that he thought Helen would like. They could have a substantial lunch, made from fresh, local ingredients, which should fortify them for their afternoon's trek. They had already done a lot of walking, but the grounds of Crathes were particularly wonderful to roam and could not be ignored.

As they pulled up to the restaurant, Helen gasped in delight. "How beautiful is this?" she exclaimed, looking at the charming stone cottage and the brilliant flowers in hanging baskets and planters. "This place looks wonderful, Matt. And I am so hungry. I don't think I have walked that much for a long time."

Matt was pleased that she was excited about the spot. He hadn't been there for a few years, but had always enjoyed the quality of the place and its beautiful setting. "I think you will like the food here, Lenny. It's all fresh and locally produced. The chefs are great – at least they have been in the past."

They were seated outside on the terrace behind the cottage, overlooking the garden and a lovely stream. It was uncharacteristically warm and windless, and the sun beating down on them felt sublime. Matt ordered a bottle of white wine. It was an Australian pino grigio, and was light and crisp but with a good body. He felt this would be just the thing for the two of them as they sat in the sun, on a terrace surrounded by flowers. They ordered the soup of the day, a hearty one of summer leeks and potatoes, followed by mains of stuffed salmon. Too full for dessert, they couldn't resist the homemade shortbread with their tea. They leaned back in their chairs, cups of tea in hand, basking in the bright sun.

"This is divine," Helen ventured, "I feel completely peaceful and content. What a great meal. Thank you for such a wonderful lunch. And morning." Helen covered her eyes with her hand to avoid squinting in the brightness as she looked over at Matt. Matt looked pretty laid back too with his eyes closed, soaking in the rays.

"You are very welcome, Lenny. It's a pleasure for me to do so, and to have your company too. But do not get too comfortable, lassie; we should be on our way soon to Crathes. Especially with this glorious weather – it will be perfect for looking at the gardens in particular. And the weather can change quickly here you know." Matt spoke quietly, and his eyes remained shut. He had a smile on his face and looked completely relaxed.

"Whenever you are ready, I am too." replied Helen. "I can't wait to see these gardens. Sarah has told me a lot about them too. She said that the garden at Crathes was meticulously planned and very formal; rather uncharacteristic of Scottish castle gardens she said."

"Yes – it is more formal than most," agreed Matt as he hoisted himself out of the chair. "I am going to visit the restroom, and then we can be on our way."

Helen nodded in agreement and decided to do the same. When she returned to the table, Matt was not yet there as he had been engaged in conversation by one of the chefs on his way back from the gent's. Helen sat down and took in the beautiful view. Out of the corner of her eye, she sensed a movement at the top of the little stream where it emerged from the woods beyond. She turned her head to look closer and saw a woman in a long green dress standing by the stream. The woman looked familiar and Helen was wondering to herself if it was someone who worked at the restaurant. However, none of the others were dressed in what seemed to Helen to be a period costume of some sort. Then the woman waved her hand. Helen scanned the area to see who she might be waving to but then realized that she was waving at her. She leaned forward to try to see who it was just as Matt returned to their table.

"Matt – do you know that person?" Helen asked. "The lady in green there by the stream. Does she work here or did we see her at one of the castles? She's waving at me." Matt looked in the direction that Helen indicated but there was nobody there.

"I don't see anyone, Helen."

Helen looked around again and then scanned the restaurant to see if this person was approaching or had gone elsewhere on the property, but there was no trace of her.

"That's odd. It seemed like she was waving to me. Oh well. Just a friendly sort I guess."

Helen felt a twinge in the pit of her stomach. She was determined to ignore it and not let anything spoil a day that was thus far so pleasant. At the same time, the sensation unnerved her because she was unused to feeling anxious about anything; at least, since she had been a child, and her friend Sarah had helped her a lot to overcome her anxieties when around other people. She pushed the feeling away as best she could, and smiled brightly at Matt.

"I'm ready to go. This was lovely. Maybe Sarah and I could come here again for lunch before I go home." Matt nodded his agreement as they walked out to the car, the pea gravel crunching under their shoes.

Chapter 8 - A Shocking Discovery

The drive to Crathes Castle from the restaurant was a short one, and as they pulled into the parking area Helen was enthralled by the spectre of a magnificent grounds and castle. The castle looked extremely well maintained – moreso than others that they had visited or driven past. And the grounds were perfectly manicured and obviously well tended. Crathes appeared very different from other castles. Perhaps it was the smooth, creamy grey walls that distinguished it from others that were mainly constructed of stone. It was both a charming and intimidating structure. The setting was certainly beautiful, and Helen immediately understood why everyone had been so impressed by the gardens. They walked up a gravel path to a side entrance where the National Trust took its entry fee and provided guided tours. So far, Helen had not taken a guided tour per say because Matt knew so much about the castles they had been to, along with their histories. He had told her that he had a general knowledge of Crathes but not with the degree of detail that he held of the others they had been to that day. Still, Helen preferred to go it alone rather than with a group. She never liked the feeling that she was part of a 'herd' as she deemed it; nor did she like to be in a position where she might have to engage in small-talk with strangers. Matt seemed to understand this about her and did not suggest that they wait for the next tour. Once they had paid their entrance fee, they began their tour of the castle.

Almost immediately upon entering the castle, Helen felt a heaviness on her shoulders. It was a sensation of pressure pushing down on her shoulders and back. *Too much wine at lunch* she thought to herself. As they progressed through the rooms on the main floor, the weight on her back intensified – almost as if she was being pushed. She shrugged her shoulders and straightened her back. Maybe it was all the driving about in the car that was doing this. She ignored it as best she could because she really wanted to focus her full attention on what she was doing, and on what Matt had to say. When they got to the dining room area, there was a group listening to the tour guide. Matt seemed very interested and joined the group. Helen listened for awhile, but caught sight of the stairwell to the next floor, and decided to continue on her own. Matt would catch up with her at some point.

The stairwell was very narrow and the stone steps were worn. They were also very close together which made Helen wonder if the original inhabitants had been small of stature. Rather on the tall side herself, she found it easier to take two steps at a time. The stairs curved around in the tower structure and it seemed to take some time to get to the next level. As she advanced, Helen noticed that the pressure on her shoulders increased, and she felt very cold suddenly. At the top of the stairs she entered a hall with doors to several rooms that she deemed to be bedrooms. Through a door at the end of the hall, she caught a glimpse of a fireplace and decided to start there. She walked into the room pulling her sweater closer as the air was really chilly despite the sunshine streaming in through the windows. She stood in the centre of the room admiring the large fireplace and hearth. In front there were four tiny chairs – children's chairs, and Helen imagined to herself that this must have been the nursery at one time. She sensed a movement behind her and turned to see a lady in a long green dress standing on the other side of the room beneath a small window. She was holding a bundle in her arms, like a baby, although there was no movement from the child.

"Oh, hello," ventured Helen. "What a lovely room. Was it the nursery at one time?" The woman nodded but did not say anything.

"Did I see you outside at the restaurant down the road?" Helen asked. Again the woman nodded. Because of the sun coming into the room, Helen could not see her face clearly, even though they were not far apart. The woman was young; probably in her teens or early twenties at most. *Not very talkative. She should be more forthcoming with information for visitors.*

"Can you tell me a little about this room and the family whose children used those chairs?"

The woman moved her arm and pointed to a desk in the corner with some brochures on it. Helen walked over to the desk and picked up a brochure. She scanned the first page and, indeed, there was information about the nursery.

"Thank you," she said, turning around, but the woman was gone. *Well, I guess I am not expected to have any questions.* Helen leaned against the wall and began to read the brochure. As she read, she felt dizzy and cold. The pressure she had felt on her shoulders intensified so much that she had to sit down.

When Matt found Helen, and saw her half slumped over, sitting in a chair in the far corner of the nursery, he was alarmed. He knew that she had a pale complexion but her face was absolutely drained of any colour at all. As he got closer, he noticed beads of perspiration on her forehead.

"Helen! What's the matter? Are you ill?" He rushed to her side. She looked up at him with both fear and sadness in her eyes. She handed him the brochure.

"My dream..." she stuttered, "this is too strange – oh my god – I can't believe it." Matt read through the brochure and was silent for a few minutes.

"God, Helen. I see what you mean. This gives me a case of the boodie fear. What a strange coincidence!"

The brochure alluded to the story of the "Green Lady of Crathes": the ghost of a young woman in a green dress or robe who sometimes appeared in the nursery room holding a child in her arms. The ghost had haunted the room for decades, causing more than one inhabitant to avoid the room in the tower. According to some historical accounts, a young woman under the protection of the ancient Laird of the castle was impregnated by one of his servants. She later gave birth to a child, but both she and the child vanished suddenly, and the servant left the estate and was never seen again. Many decades later, the fireplace in the nursery was undergoing repairs when workmen lifted the hearthstone and uncovered the bones of a young child in a complete and perfect skeleton. The mystery of what happened to the girl and the baby had never been solved, although there had been much speculation. When the skelton was discovered, many assumed that it was the remains of the baby, and that the "green lady" ghost was its mother.

Helen felt emotionally exhausted and quite shocked. She continued to wonder to herself whether this discovery – what she had just witnessed and read – was somehow connected to her disturbing dream on her first night in Scotland. She struggled with the notion because this was not something she had ever taken an interest in or sought out. She had had friends who were intrigued by belief in life after death, restless spirits, but she had never given it a great deal of thought herself. Somehow, though, she knew instinctively that what she had experienced was for real, and that it was connected to her recent dreams. The larger questions for Helen were – why and why her? It was difficult to wrap her mind around it all.

"Lenny, let me get you outside for some fresh air. I think you've had enough for today." Matt looked very concerned as he helped her out of the chair and wrapped his arm around her waist for support as they left the room and navigated their way down the stairs. She was shaken by the incident and appreciated Matt's taking charge and getting her out of there.

Matt and Helen drove home in silence. He had steered her out of the castle and straight to the car. She continued to feel quite dizzy, and laid her head back on the seat with her eyes closed. Matt was concerned and, at the same time, trying to make sense out of what had just happened. Of course he had heard stories about many ghosts haunting most of the castles all over Scotland; one could not grow up there without knowledge of this. He had never experienced anything himself, except for once, as a child, shortly after his mother had died, when he felt her presence in his room. He had cried himself to sleep one night, missing terribly the comfort of being cuddled in her arms. He had awoken to the sensation of someone smoothing his hair from his brow and kissing him lightly on the cheek. He had felt loved and secure, and had opened his eyes sleepily to look at his mother, and then the realization that it had been a dream hit him like a ton of bricks. He had begun to cry again, his little heart breaking, when suddenly he felt a calm and peacefulness sweep like a wave through his body. He had stared into the darkness of the room and could see nothing but the outlines of his furniture, but he sensed that she was there with him. He had gone back to sleep feeling happier, and after that, though he continued to miss her, he did not experience the gut-wrenching sorrow that had previously enveloped him after her death.

He pondered Helen's dream and the meeting she had had in the nursery at Crathes. It all seemed too unlikely; however, she had been completely unaware of any of the stories or history of the castle – and, probably, uninterested in this sort of thing. She was also clearly affected by her encounter, so it seemed unlikely that such a logical and scientific-minded person would imagine something like this. Matt was not sure what he should do next, but decided that the first step was to get Helen back to Ian and Sarah's and get some whisky into her. Also, he thought that Sarah needed to be told what had happened. She would be able to help Helen more effectively than himself.

Helen rallied herself as they pulled into the driveway. She was feeling a bit better, although still light-headed. *God, he must think I am a really strange – if he had doubts before I have just certified it. He looks so concerned; I've scared him. He probably thinks I have some mental health issues now.*

"Thanks for looking after me, Matt – I feel so silly. Maybe I had too much wine at lunch; I'm not used to drinking much you know." Helen tried to lighten the tension and forced a smile.

"No worries, Lenny. Don't feel silly. I am glad you are feeling a bit better; your colour is coming back and I am relieved to see it. I was going to suggest a whisky, but I think maybe a strong cup of tea will do you more good. Let's get Sarah and she what she thinks about all of this."

"Good idea, Matt. And thanks. Not just for a great day out – really it was wonderful, and I feel like I wrecked it for you. If you are up to it, I want to go back and walk around those gardens – really, I mean it."

Matt was looking a bit skeptical at the prospect of returning to Crathes, and he really seemed to care about her wellbeing.

"I admit that I have had quite a shock, and my reaction was textbook-don't forget, I am a doctor after all. But I am over it now and I feel like I must get to the bottom of this. And, at the very least, I have to see those storied gardens that everyone raves about! Let's go find Sarah." Helen was desperate to lighten the atmosphere, despite the fact that she still felt rather discombobulated. She had also decided, enroute, that she must uncover the reason for the connection between her dream, what she saw and experienced and whatever it meant.

Chapter 9 – Ghost of the Lady in the Green Dress

When Helen and Matt told Sarah about what had happened in the Crathes nursery room, her eyes widened with incredulity. She shivered at the thought that there was some kind of connection between Helen's nightmares about the child's hand coming out of the hearth at her home, and the discovery of the sad and horrific account about the child's bones found in the hearth in the nursery. Helen was obviously and justifiably upset by the whole experience, and Sarah wanted to reassure her, but wasn't quite sure how to go about it in this instance. She had never had any sort of experience like this and, while she was cognizant of the rich history of spirits in Scotland – indeed all over Great Britain – she was more bemused by it than anything else. She knew too that Helen was not a believer in ghosts, so the entire situation was rather puzzling for her and, she could see, to Helen as well. They were still discussing it all when Ian arrived home with the boys, having collected them at school on his way home.

"Well. I did not expect to see you two here until later," he exclaimed upon entering the kitchen. "I thought you would be walking the grounds at Crathes about now."

Matt decided it would be best to take Ian out of the room and let him know what had happened. Helen had had enough excitement for one day, and he suspected that Ian might say something to upset her further.

"Let's the two of us go have a whisky in the den, brother, " Matt suggested, jumping up to steer Ian out of the kitchen. "It's not often I get the opportunity to talk to you alone, and I think the ladies would like a chance to talk without us impeding their conversation. Are the boys doing their homework? When they're done, we could play some footy – I could use the exercise." Ian looked very pleased to have Matt take him over and nodded in agreement, winking at Sarah as he left the room.

"We'll get dinner ready, and I will check on the boys and send them to you when they've finished," offered Sarah. "Lenny, I am just going to see if baby is awake from her nap and bring her down here with us. You have your tea and relax. I will just be a minute or two."

Helen smiled and nodded, appreciative of a little respite however brief. She was feeling much better, the tea had helped, but was still uneasy with the events of the day. *I need to talk to someone who can make some sense of this for me. But whom? This is too creepy and sad and disturbing. And why me of all people? Especially since I am here to have a vacation. Poor Sari – she doesn't need to be worrying about me either. What the hell! Maybe I should just forget it and stay away from castles, and Crathes in particular!* The thoughts were still running through her mind when Sarah returned.

"Where is my little darling?" she asked Sarah when her friend returned without the baby.

"Oh, she is with her daddy and Uncle Matt. He wanted her and she is entertaining them both. She is such a delightful happy child." Sari was pleased that Ian had called to her when she came downstairs with the baby.

"She is a doll – everyone loves her to bits. I am so sorry for this, Sari. I don't want you to worry or for my visit to become a nuisance. I have no idea where this all came from or why. My god! Have I lost my mind suddenly? Have I been working too hard and this is some kind of weird manifestation of stress? Bloody h-e-double hockey sticks! The problem is – and I keep seeing it in my head – I saw her in that room. And the way she looked at me – like she was pleading for me to help her. But with what? Honestly, I do not know what to do about it. If anything."

Sarah noticed that as she spoke, her friend had lined up her cup, the creamer and sugar in front of her like a little fortress. She smiled, recognizing her friend's outward manifestation of self protection against the world.

"Lenny – don't be silly. You should know that I want you here more than anything, and nothing you could do could change my mind. I am just sorry that you are having experiences that are obviously out of the ordinary and upsetting you so much. And of course they would. Anybody would be upset by the dreams you have had, not to mention an encounter with a famous ghost. We'll figure something out together." Sarah gave her friend a hug.

"Why don't you go have a nice bath, and I will get dinner going. You just relax. You have been walking all over today as well; you must be tired. And here, take this with you!" Sarah poured a glass of wine for Helen. As ever, Helen listened to Sarah and decided to do exactly as she suggested. She was relieved that nobody was making a huge fuss about what had happened, although she would have loved to be a fly on the wall in the den to hear what Ian would say about it all.

She came down later to find the children having their dinner in the kitchen and the table set for four in the dining room. Sarah was busily feeding the baby and chatting with the boys. The men had gone upstairs to freshen up for dinner.

"Oh good – you're looking refreshed. Matt has gone up to do the same and I thought the four of us could eat a bit later."

"I am feeling much better, Sari, thanks. Good idea. Can I help? Why don't I take over when you are finished feeding the baby, and you can have a chance to relax yourself?"

"Thanks Lenny, I will take you up on that. Ian should be back down shortly and he can help. I think the homework is done, but I would like the boys to do a bit of reading. Maybe they could each read something to their Aunty Lenny? How about that boys?" Sarah grinned at them, knowing that they did not like to read aloud but would do it for Lenny. They agreed to the plan with enthusiasm.

When Ian came down later, he found Helen with the boys and the baby in the parlour. Miraculously, the boys were taking turns reading aloud to her from a library book they had grudgingly agreed to borrow to placate their pesky parents' obsession with the importance of reading. He chuckled to himself, and had a feeling of contentment in the knowledge that his children had two other people who they trusted and loved – Helen and Matt. He was feeling a bit more optimistic than usual, and he couldn't help but wonder if it was because his brother was around more lately. Sarah had also been happier with having her dear friend around as well. For the first time he felt that it was okay to include others in the world of his family. That it was safe to do so. That Matt and Helen could be relied upon.

He wasn't quite sure what to make of Helen's experience at Crathes, however, and it was certainly an odd coincidence that she had had the nightmare she did before visiting the place. Neither he nor Sarah had been aware of the particulars of the discovery under the hearth there. He wondered what Helen would want to do about it if anything at all.

The next morning Matt left for Edinburgh to meet with a couple from New York who were interested in purchasing several of his paintings. He planned to return on the weekend, and to take Helen back to Crathes if that is what she wished to do. In the meantime, as Matt had suggested, Helen would go to the main library in Aberdeen to see if she could find anything that referenced the information about the child's bones being found in the nursery's hearth at Crathes. He also suggested that she call the local office of the National Trust to see if they knew of any sources that Helen might access for more information about the matter.

Once Ian and the children left for the day, Helen and Sarah sat down to have a coffee in the morning sun while the baby went down for a nap. It was Betty's day to clean and she had arrived punctually and set to work in the kitchen, so they had moved outside so as not to be in the way. They enjoyed the quiet time together and the opportunity to just be with each other – talking or not.

"Why don't I drive you into town, and I can take the baby for a walk and do a bit of shopping while you are at the library?" Sarah offered, when Helen told her about Matt's suggestions. "It's another lovely day, and it would clear the house for Betty anyway."

"I would love that, Sari. We could take baby for lunch afterwards too. Instead of calling the National Trust, do you think we could pop by their office? Since we will be in town anyway?" Helen asked. Sarah nodded in agreement, and they decided to finish their coffee and get themselves ready so that they could leave as soon as little Helen woke up.

It was late morning by the time Sarah dropped Helen off at the library and they decided to rendezvous at a restaurant in a couple of hours. The library staff was friendly and helpful, and directed Helen to the local history section where she was able to access historical accounts and records of castles in the area near Aberdeen. Within this section, there were also some records of ghost sightings, and, in particular, various renditions of the ghost of the lady wearing the green dress or the "green lady" seen at Crathes Castle. Helen was disappointed, however, that there was not a lot of detail. Generally, she found limited descriptions of the sightings, and various speculations on those who the ghosts might represent. There was a passage about the ghost of the lady in green within the historical records of Crathes castle, and about the bones of the child being discovered in the nursery hearth. However, there was little new information from that documented in the brochure given out at the castle.

Essentially there were a couple of theories about the bones in the hearth. One was that a young girl, who had been taken in by the Lord and Lady at the time, had become pregnant by one of the servants. Both the servant and the girl had mysteriously disappeared. Some opined that the servant had killed the child and the girl and then run away. Another theory was that the Lady had become enraged at the situation and had killed the mother and child, and sent the servant away. In any case, the only bones discovered had been those of the child in the nursery hearth. As Helen continued to leaf through the books and documents, in a book called "The Ghosthunters Almanac", she stopped at a notation about Crathes that, for her, was a more poignant reference – given her own encounter with the ghost. As she read, she shivered, recalling her own experience in the castle's nursery. *Good god – it's the ghost that I saw - the Green Lady of Crathes. She glides across the room and lifts up a child from the fireplace, then both disappear.* Helen read on that the ghost may have haunted the area centuries prior to Crathes being built, and some had speculated that she may have been a jealous murderess. However, later when under repair, the skeletons of both a woman and baby were discovered by workmen in the hearth of the fireplace in the room that was known to be haunted.

The passage further revealed that others had witnessed the apparition, and Helen assumed that the 'haunted room' referenced must have been the same room in which she had seen and spoken to the young lady in the green dress holding the baby. Apparently some members of the family who had owned the property for generations had also been frightened by this ghost. There was some comfort in knowing that she was not the only one who had encountered it, although she continued to feel somewhat embarrassed for having had the experience. Intellectually, the idea of it happening was just too difficult to reconcile with her sense of reality.

Helen photocopied the passage from the book so she could show it to Sarah and Matt. She found nothing more in the library, but got the address for the local office of the National Trust. The librarian told Helen that there was usually a local historian on the premises and that he might be able to shed some light on the story behind the existence of ghosts at Crathes.

Sarah was waiting for Helen at a restaurant down the street from the library. As it was already getting closer to mid afternoon and Baby's nap time, instead of lunch, they decided to have a quick cup of tea and some scones, then make a short stop at the National Trust office before heading home. Sarah waited in the car while Helen went into the office. There was a long counter and behind it were three people seated behind large wooden desks. Helen stood at the counter for a couple of minutes without eliciting any interest or attention from anyone. Finally, she cleared her throat and ventured her request.

"Good afternoon." she said quietly. "I have a couple of questions I would like to ask about one of the castles in the area."

A balding, middle aged man looked up at her over his glasses. The others continued to stare at the papers on their desks.

"Yes?" he responded, somewhat impatiently. "Which castle would that be, madam?"

"Crathes Castle. Thank you."

Helen was uncomfortable. Obviously visitors were not entirely welcome. He stared intently at her as if waiting.

"I want to ask if there was someone here who might be able to tell me about the ghost there…." she stammered out, feeling her face flushing with embarrassment.

"Let me guess, madam…the ghost of the lady in the green dress?" he asked, rolling his eyes and sniffing.

"Yes! Exactly. Do you have any information about her? I visited the castle a few days ago and I, um, had an experience. So, I am interested in finding out more about the ghost – who she is – and why she is there," Helen continued, rather taken aback by his demeanor towards her.

"Well, madam. If I had a pound for every green lady ghost story, I would be a wealthy man." he sniffed again, rolling his eyes at her once more.

"There really isn't much to the story other that it is a story that seems to be propagated by visitors who tour our castles in search of ghostly encounters. Ghosts do not exist except in the minds of those who choose to believe in them. The 'green lady' ghost is all over Scotland. Very common story. Nothing to it, madam. Is there anything else I can help you with, madam?"

"Oh. No. Thank you. Sorry to have bothered you." said Helen. She turned quickly and left the office. *What an ass! Thanks for making me feel like an idiot.* She got into the car and sat quietly.

Sarah took one look at Helen's face and knew she was not happy.

"Whatever happened in there, Lenny? Did they know of anything useful?"

"No. I am just another stupid tourist asking silly questions about ghosts. God, I feel like a complete idiot."

Helen buckled her seatbelt and sighed. "They were not very interested or helpful, and I guess they have had too many enquires about this sort of thing. They couldn't have been more unfriendly though, Sari, especially the officious little man in there."

"I am sorry, Lenny. Some are just not that welcoming to those they consider 'outsiders'. What they need to get a grip on is that their jobs and the economy here is completely benefited by visitors to the area. I should have gone in with you. I have a good mind to call the head office and complain. Really, the cheek! Who do they think they are?" Sarah was furious. This wasn't the first time that her visitors had encountered a surly local. Her reaction and inclination to go into the office and give them a piece of her mind made Helen laugh.

"Oh Sari. Don't worry about it. It's not that important. You really don't have to be looking out for me all the time," smiled Helen. "Let's get Baby home and I will show you what I found at the library. Now, you should know that they were very nice and helpful at the library, and seemed to take me quite seriously when I talked to them about the ghost at Crathes. So, there you are, not everyone here is rude to strangers; some are actually very nice."

Sarah composed herself, and as they drove into Aberdeenshire, Helen focused her attention on the baby and entertained her until they arrived home.

Once the baby was fed and down for her nap, Sarah and Helen looked over the photocopied pages. They decided to discuss the findings with Matt and that another trip to Crathes was indeed in order. This time, Sarah wanted to go as well. She had been to Crathes years ago; Matt had taken her on a tour of castles shortly after she had arrived in Scotland. But she had not gone beyond the gardens and the main floor areas of the property. She decided that she would accompany Helen to the nursery room, and to ask some questions of the National Trust employees who staffed the reception areas at the castle. Probably they would know more than the little twit at the office in town.

Sarah also wanted to talk to Ian about the ghost at Crathes. Maybe he knew something. Or maybe there was someone at the university who would know something more about Crathes and its history. She would have to tread carefully though, as she did not want to create a situation where Ian and Helen might get into it. If only they could get along. But Sarah felt instinctively that Ian would help if given a chance. She would enlist Matt's assistance in facilitating a discussion with Ian about a connection between

Helen's dream and her experience at Crathes. Clearly Helen was determined to find some sort of resolution to the puzzle of her dream and its relevance to the Crathes ghost.

Chapter 10 – Return to Crathes

Matt was anxious to get back to Aberdeenshire. He was both intrigued and worried about Helen's experience and the effect it was having on her. She was definitely struggling with the notion of the existence of spirits, and that there was a very real, non-physical dimension to life. And to death. Matt, himself, had never given any of this sort of thing much thought, albeit it's prevalence within the cultural fabric of Scotland. He simply accepted that it was possible likely because the concept of the existence of a spiritual world was a normal part of living in Scotland; it was a part of the rich lore and history of the country. To him, it wasn't scary or odd. On the contrary, his only experience had been tremendously comforting to him. He could imagine circumstances, however, where this might not be the case.

His meeting with the American tourists had gone well and he had sold four paintings to them. They were from New York and seemed to be well-connected within the arts community there, and wanted to have Matt bring some of his works for a show in a gallery in Manhattan. Matt was flattered, of course, and agreed to consider the possibility. He loved the Americans he had met over the years, at the various Edinburgh galleries where his work was shown. They were a bit on the brash side; however, he admired their confidence and forthrightness. Anyway, it was something to think about. He wasn't sure how Ian would react if he decided to do it. The timing would have to be right, particularly because he was committed to taking on more responsibility for the family properties and finances. He did not want to disappoint Ian – not again. He had seen the relief in Ian's face at the thought of lightening his workload. Poor Ian. He had always worked so hard and had so many responsibilities. Matt could not let him down –

not this time. He could hardly wait for the weekend to get back to the house and see them all. For the first time in many years, Matt felt a strong sense of belonging and family. Becoming the baby's Godfather meant so much to him; he was grateful to Sarah and Ian for including him in such an intimate way with their family. This last couple of weeks had been very special, and different in a way and for reasons he could not articulate yet. It was almost as if he had been brought back from the brink of terminal 'old-bachelorhood' into the close bond of family. He knew that Sarah had made it happen, and that both he and Ian should be grateful to her for this. Wise Sarah; she was his sister in every sense, and also provided him with the care and consideration of a loving mother. She made him feel at home and at peace when he was there. He also now sensed that his brother was pleased and happy for this new development in their relationship.

    He called Sarah to tell her he would arrive later on Friday evening and to see what she and Helen had decided about further Crathes excursions. Sarah suggested that perhaps the whole family could go on Saturday afternoon, but that they could discuss a definitive plan when he got there. She told him briefly about the trip to the library and National Trust office in Aberdeen. She also mentioned her desire to bring Ian into the discussion. Matt sensed that this would be tricky, given Helen's and Ian's inability to get along, but he agreed it would be worth a try as Ian would likely have some good ideas about how to proceed. That was if Ian would take it seriously; this was the question and the risk in including him. Maybe he should clear it with Helen first; otherwise, she might feel insulted. *No*, he thought, *better to just make a casual suggestion.*

Matt arrived at the Wallace's just as the boys were headed to bed. They were excited to see him, but disappointed that it was their bedtime. Matt placated them by offering to read a couple of stories to them in their room before they went to sleep. He was tired from the drive, but wanted to spend the time with them too. And he was inwardly thrilled to see the delight in their faces at his suggestion. Ian and Helen were tidying the kitchen and chatting amicably, while Sarah took the baby for her bath and bedtime preparations. In Matt's view, this Friday evening, the Wallace household was a scene of domestic bliss and harmony – moreso than before Helen's arrival. He wasn't sure why this was the case, but guessed that Sarah was less tired and happier herself with her friend there to help her and to keep her company. He would really have to make an effort to be there more often, especially after Helen's departure in two short weeks. He could not believe how quickly the time was going by, and he had to admit to himself that he would be sorry to see Helen go – ghostly preoccupations notwithstanding. He enjoyed her company and, moreso, appreciated her obvious love for Sarah and his nephews and niece.

When he came downstairs after reading to the boys, after finding nobody in the kitchen or sitting room, he found Ian, Sarah and Helen sitting outside in the garden. It was a lovely clear evening with a star-studded sky, and the air was crisp and refreshing, and unusually calm.

"Matty – here's a chair waiting for you," smiled his brother, "and a glass of wine. We thought maybe you had fallen asleep with the boys." Ian gestured for him to sit in the chair nearest himself, poured some wine for Matt and topped up the others' glasses.

"I almost did!" laughed Matt. "Those two had me read four of their favourite stories. And then I had to tell them all about my trip to town. I also had to promise to get up and play with them in the morning too – which I am only too happy to do. They are such good lads."

"Thank you for reading to them, Matty," interjected Sarah, "they love it so much – especially when it's you or Helen. You must be tired from your drive too; it's so good of you to do it."

"My pleasure and privilege, Sarah – really. I love every minute possible with those boys. Now; what is the plan for tomorrow? Are we headed to Crathes for the afternoon? It should be a nice day for roaming the gardens. Helen – are you still wanting to go and do some further investigation? Sarah tells me that you had some luck at the library and not so much at the National Trust office?" Matt tried his best to keep the tone matter-of-fact so as to raise the subject in front of Ian in a casual way for Helen's sake.

"Investigation? Are you investigating something, Helen? Does this have something to do with your ghost?" asked Ian.

"I know you think it is nonsensical, Ian," Helen returned, "…but, yes, I do want to find out more about the ghost in the nursery at Crathes. I am not sure what to make of it all. I have never had dreams or an experience like this before. Maybe its nothing, but I can't help but feel there is something I must do. I can't explain it which is very frustrating for me."

Helen was serious about getting some sort of resolution to this situation – whatever it was. She had decided to keep an open mind and see what happened. She could do that. After all, this was how one made discoveries in research: scientific methodology combined with imagination and a willingness to be open to the unexpected.

Why should her approach be different in this case? Minus the science, of course, but her interest had been ignited.

"I think we should all go tomorrow," proposed Sarah. "We can go after lunch. The gardens will be lovely and the boys can run off some steam. I want Helen to show me where she saw the ghost, and to help her get some information if possible."

"Well, why not?" replied Ian, enjoying the looks of surprise on the others' faces at his easy agreement. "Indeed, the weather is supposed to be good. I think it would be a fun trip for the boys and a nice outing for the baby. Besides, I haven't been to one of our castles for years. In fact, I don't think I have ever been to the Crathes Castle before; it's time I went."

"Good thinking my brother, and I agree with you," ventured Matt, amazed that Ian was willing to go, and wasn't making light of the reason for the trip. "It's settled then. We'll go for the afternoon. Helen, why don't I make the enquiries with the staff while you and Sarah go up to the nursery room?"

"I'll stay outside in the gardens with the baby, and let the boys run around," offered Ian.

Sarah and Helen looked at each other and both agreed readily to the offered scenario. Both were stunned, in a pleasant way, by Ian's response to the suggested outing. Helen was a bit suspicious and wondered why he was being so cooperative; it wasn't his normal style. *Maybe he is making an effort*, she thought to herself, *and none too soon.* Whatever the reason, she could see that Sarah was relieved and pleased, and she appreciated Ian's willingness to go along with them, and to offer to supervise the kids while they sought out some further information about the green lady and her child.

After a leisurely morning at the house, Ian and Matt cleaned up the kitchen after lunch while Sarah and Helen got the children ready for the excursion to Crathes. The boys were very excited to be going, especially since their daddy and their uncle would be with them too. It wasn't often that Ian accompanied them to anything – whether it was for sports activities, shopping or visits to friends' homes. He was always at the university or in his study; Sarah took them to everything. The fact that the whole family was going somewhere together was a real treat for them. Ian was pleased too. He did have a lot of work to do, but it could wait for now. He had noticed how much happier Sarah had been over the past couple of weeks and was astute enough to see that she was in desperate need of some rest and diversion from her daily routine. And it was lovely for him to see the delight in his boys' eyes when they heard that he was going too.

He felt a pang of guilt when it struck him how little time he had spent with them. He had never wanted to be like his own father in the sense that work came first to the exclusion of leisure time with family. He had been pleased when his father insisted that he help him with estate matters; however, the focus had been on the work rather than on spending time together. As a result, he had always been somewhat intimidated by his father, and had never felt close to him. Ian did not want this to be the case for him and his boys. He loved his sons, and Sarah was doing such a fine job with them, but he knew it was time he established a closer relationship with them. If he didn't do it now, it would be too late soon as their interest in his attention would not be there once they hit their teenage years.

They arrived at Crathes Castle in the early afternoon. It was a bright day with some real warmth in the sun and a few cumulus clouds floating by every once in awhile. Though it was summer, sweaters were required, particularly when the sun disappeared behind a fluffy cloud. Nathan and Jonah made a beeline for the grand lawn that stretched out below the castle. It was lined by trees and provided a perfect spot for them to run its length in a race. Ian took the baby from her car seat and placed her gently in her pram that Matt had retrieved from the trunk of the car. He adjusted the back so that the little darling could look about. Sarah and Helen fussed over her to ensure that she was secure and had the right amount of blanketing. She was a content little baby and cooed with delicious baby sounds as she stared up at four adoring faces.

"Okay lassies – she is fine and properly ensconced," smiled Ian. "Off you go to do your 'investigation'. I will take over from here with the children."

"Thank you, dear," said Sarah, and kissed him on the cheek. "We won't be that long. Keep a close eye on the boys – you can't take your eyes off of them even for a second, Ian."

"Don't worry, love. I've got it. You enjoy yourself. I hope you find your ghost!" he replied, smiling at the other three.

"Thanks brother, let's go ladies."

Matt nodded at Ian and quickly steered Sarah and Helen towards the castle, noticing a look of displeasure on Helen's face at Ian's comment. Poor Ian – he was always sticking his foot in it. Sarah noticed it too and cringed a bit hoping that Helen would let the comment pass without taking offence.

As soon as they paid their entrance fee, Matt began enquiring about whom he could talk to about the history of the ghost. Helen took Sarah's arm and led her up the stairs to the nursery room. There was a fairly large group of tourists in the room with the guide as they arrived at the door. Helen was feeling the same heaviness on her shoulders, and a sudden chill that made her zip up her sweater. Sarah was listening intently to the guide as he talked about the room and its use in past years. She moved up and stood behind the group while Helen waited by the door for the group to move on.

"Help me!"

From behind her, someone whispered loudly into Helen's ear. Helen spun around quickly to see who needed her assistance to see the outline of a young woman just down the hall at the top of the stairs. She moved slowly towards Helen,

"Please - help me," she pleaded.

As she came closer, Helen saw that the woman, in a long green gown, carried a small child wrapped in a blanket. The child's head, with its light blonde curls, dangled limply from the curve of her arm. Helen could see that the woman was crying and in distress as her misty figure moved toward and disappeared into the wall behind the fireplace. Helen couldn't move and she couldn't speak.

"Lenny, what's wrong?" asked a concerned Sarah. "You look like you have seen a ghost! Oh. Have you? Again? Lenny, come and sit down!"

Sarah led Helen over to the lone adult chair in the room and sat her down. Helen was a bit dazed as she looked around the room and suddenly realized that the tour group was gone.

"Did you see her, Sari? Did you see her – the baby – did you see the baby?" Helen was distraught. "She is here. She wants help."

"No, Lenny. I don't see anything," responded Sarah softly, sounding disappointed. "You saw her again? Really? Where exactly?"

Helen recounted what she had seen and the words spoken to her by the apparition. She felt like she was in a trance-like state and the pressure on her back and shoulders was intense. It was hard to think straight.

"Let's get out of here," shivered Sarah, when she heard what had transpired.

"Sari – go if you like, but I have to stay here and see if she comes back. I need to know why this is happening to me – to understand why she is revealing herself to me...what it is that she wants...."

"I don't want to leave you alone here, Lenny. I am going to get Matt and come right back. You just sit here and wait for me; I will be two minutes."

Sarah left quickly to find Matt. She was frightened for Helen, but didn't quite know what to do when Helen refused to go with her. It was all so strange. This didn't happen to normal people; or, did it? She went quickly down the steep stone steps and hurried around the main floor of the castle looking for Matt. She couldn't find him anywhere. *Damn. Where is he?* she thought. Looking out the entrance she saw Matt talking to Ian at the end of the walk. Ian had the baby in his arms, but the boys were not visible to her. Somewhat alarmed, Sarah ran out to where they stood, calling out to Matt.

"Matty, come with me – quickly. Lenny's in a state; she's had another encounter with the ghost. Come quickly." Sarah was out of breath. "Ian – where are the boys?"

"They were right here a minute ago," replied Ian, looking around and surprised that he couldn't see them anywhere. He sensed he was in trouble now for taking his eyes off of them. "They're not far, I am sure – don't you worry."

"I told you to watch them closely, Ian; they get playing and lose track of where they are and the time." Sarah was frustrated and torn between wanting to look for her sons and tending to Helen.

"Ian, why don't you come with me to the nursery and leave Sarah here with the children?" Matt suggested, feeling sorry for his brother and a bit guilty for having distracted him. They had been discussing the information that Matt had gotten from the on-site historian. There hadn't been much additional information to what Helen had already obtained; however, the man had some interesting speculations and, moreover, had not balked at the idea of the ghost being present. He, himself, had seen her a few times late at night when he had been locking up. Not at close range, but he had seen her looking out the nursery window, and, on another occasion, going up the stairs. He was a believer in its existence. Before Ian could respond to Matt, Nathan and Jonah came running up to hug their mother. She scolded them for having run off on their father, but was obviously relieved.

"Yes, Ian. You go with Matty. I'll take the boys for their tea at the cafeteria. The baby needs her bottle anyway. Do you mind?" Sarah looked at Ian and he could see that she wanted to stay with the children.

"Not at all, dear," he replied, glad to be out of the doghouse for losing sight of the boys. "Don't worry about Helen, we'll go and retrieve her. We'll join you in a bit." With that, he and Matt hurried into the building and up the stairs to the nursery. As they reached the top of the stairs, they could hear Helen's voice from the nursery. Walking into the room, Ian stopped suddenly and stared at the fireplace. Helen was standing on one side of it and, on the other side was the figure of a young woman in a green dress leaning over the hearth. It was as if he was seeing her through a transparent whitish film. She was either picking up or laying down the small body of a child. And she was weeping. Helen was talking to her, asking, "What do you want? What do you want from me? What help can I give you?"

Matt looked at Helen and then at Ian, realizing that Ian was looking in the same direction as Helen. Helen was speaking to someone, but Matt could not see anyone there. It was obvious from the look on Ian's face, he could see something or someone – to whomever it was that Helen was speaking. Helen turned to look at them. She knew instantly that Ian could see what she did. She turned back to the hearth to see the figure fading into nothing.

"Please….don't leave. Please tell me what you want. Why are you here? What happened to your baby?"

But the figures of the woman and her child faded into the hearth and were gone. Helen began to cry silently, the tears streaming down her cheeks. Matt rushed over to her. Ian could not move. He was riveted to the spot. He could not believe what he had just witnessed. *Bloody hell. What to do now.* He shivered and felt chilled to the bone.

"Ian – let's get Helen downstairs. Come Helen."

Matt coaxed her out of the room and Ian followed closely behind. As they went down the stairs, the pressure on Helen's shoulders decreased and she felt lighter once they stepped outside.

"I'm so sorry," she stammered, wiping her eyes. "I don't know what came over me. I felt so overwhelmingly sad. Ian – you saw her didn't you? I could see that you saw something!"

"Yes, Helen, I did." Ian murmured. "I certainly did. I need a strong drink of something, brother. And quickly."

The three went and collected Sarah and the children from the castle cafeteria. As the boys had one last race on the common, Matt told Sarah what had transpired in the nursery. They decided to call it a day and to go home. As they did not want to discuss any of this in front of the children, they decided to put off any discussion until after dinner. Sarah was shocked to hear that Ian saw what Helen had seen, and wondered what his reaction would be to the experience.

Chapter 11 - A Mother's Wish

It had been a fairly silent ride home from Crathes. The children dozed off shortly after they packed up and left; the boys were tired from running about in the fresh air. The others rode in kind of a dazed silence. Helen was emotionally spent, and Ian was too stunned from the experience in the nursery to say much. Once home, they all pitched in to prepare supper and to get the children ready for bed. Ian and Matt brought in some wood and got a fire going in the sitting room. They played some board games with the boys while Helen and Sarah bathed and fed the baby, and put her to bed. Matt took the boys up to bed when the girls came downstairs, and when he returned the others were settled in with glasses of wine or whisky.

"Pour me one of those, will you Ian?" asked Matt. The first gulp of whisky went down pretty easily, and after another couple, he felt himself relaxing. It appeared the others were appreciating the same experience. They were staring into the fire and the room was silent for several minutes before Ian brought up the inevitable.

"Well, dear ones, I have no idea what to make of what happened today. It was a first for me. Helen, I don't know what to say to you about it…except that I am sorry for poking fun at you before. It is an inexplicable thing. On the one hand, intellectually, I can't fathom it; yet, on the other, I know it to be true – I saw her too!" Ian trembled slightly as he spoke, recalling the spectre of the ghost and her child fading into the hearth of the fireplace.

"Thank you, Ian – for understanding how it has affected me," murmured Helen, looking appreciative of his comment. She gathered some cushions around her, and continued, "I am completely puzzled as to why I am seeing her, and what she wants from me? I still cannot believe that I am actually considering that there is something I must do – for a ghost! Yet, I know that there is something I must do….that there is a reason for all of this." Helen shook her head and looked at Matt. "Matt, Ian told us what you found out. It is some comfort to know that the fellow at Crathes has seen her too. Did he have any ideas about why she's there – other than the storyline we've already heard?"

"Nothing," Matt replied. "But he didn't bat an eye when I told him what you had seen in the nursery. He – Geordie's his name – was very matter-of-fact about it all. He did say that there have been other tourists, and some of the staff, who have felt uneasy or thought that they had seen something in that room or on the staircase. His own view, and he firmly believes this, is that some people are simply more sensitive to what he surmises as 'vibrations' from those who have passed but have yet to resolve something before they can progress into the world of 'life after death' if you will. He also said that if you get the opportunity, you should ask it directly what it wants. It might answer."

"If you don't mind my opinion, Helen," ventured Ian, "I think you will have to suspend your disbelief in this instance. Instead of trying to rationalize the experience, we just have to remove the prospect of a logical explanation, accept that it is real, and act – or don't act – from that premise. Does that make any sense to you?" As he spoke, both Sarah and Matt nodded in agreement.

"Amazingly, it does make sense to me," replied Helen, feeling relieved on two counts; firstly, that there had been sightings by others, and, secondly, that Ian seemed to understand precisely the conundrum within her about it all.

"And you saw her too – which I have to admit, shocks the hell out of me, but also validates her existence for me. What I still don't know is what am I supposed to do about it?"

"Maybe there is nothing to do, Lenny," offered Sarah, smiling intently at her friend, and feeling intensely relieved that Ian was taking a helpful approach. "Maybe this is just what she does…she's stuck, like Robert said, and will always be there. You don't have to do anything."

"I guess that is one way of looking at it, but I just get the sense that there is something to be done; that I must help her. I don't know why, but it's a strong feeling." Helen looked forlorn as she expressed herself. She was really laying bare her emotional response to what had been happening.

"Do you think that it could be that this feeling comes from the fact that you are a doctor?" suggested Matt. "You are so used to helping people in distress – to finding out what their ailment is and providing a remedy? In this case, perhaps there is no remedy that you could provide – even if you wanted to – I mean, really, what can you do for a ghost? But it is your natural and, might I add, professional inclination to help a being in obvious distress, Lenny. I tend to agree with Geordie; the ghost is there – always has been and always will be – no action is necessary."

"Well, perhaps you are all right. As usual, I am probably focusing too much on it. And you do make a good point, Matt. All of you are right, and I appreciate your thoughts on it." Helen sighed and poured herself another glass of wine. "Actually, I do feel quite relieved at the prospect that I don't have to do anything about it. I am just another one of those tourists who have seen the ghost of the green lady with her child. That's it. Why am I driving myself crazy? I do think this is the right approach. That's it then. Oh my god. If I wasn't so embarrassed, it would be a great story to tell about my trip to Scotland."

Helen laughed as she said this, and relaxed into her cushions. It was going to be okay after all. No need for anything further on this subject. She resolved to spend the final two weeks of her visit just doing that – visiting. They talked for awhile longer as the fire dwindled and went out. Exhausted and sleepy from the wine, Helen excused herself and went to bed. The others followed soon thereafter.

"Helen…Helen…"

Helen wakened as she heard her name whispered into her ear. She was groggy with sleep and struggled to open her eyes. She squinted into the darkness and could see nothing.

"Sari – is that you?" she murmured. There was no immediate reply, so she turned over to go back to sleep.

"Help me please, Helen."

This time she recognized the voice. As she opened her eyes and looked up, a shimmering outline of the woman was at the end of her bed. Helen rubbed her eyes and tried to sit up, but she felt as if she was paralysed.

"What can I do? What do you want?" she stammered. It was difficult to get the words out, as if her mouth was full of marbles. The woman pointed to the fireplace.

"I need your help, ma'am, please help me…my baby…I want my baby."

The apparition was sobbing and in distress. Helen couldn't move. She felt that she must be dreaming and tried to wake herself up. Then she remembered what Matt had said about asking questions.

"You have your baby. I've seen you with the baby. What can I do? Why are you here with me?" It was so hard to get the words out and seemed to take forever.

"I want to take her with me, ma'am," wailed the girl, "but I cannot. Please – I must have her blessed, ma'am. Otherwise we will be forever parted. Please ma'am, help me...I need your help. Nobody will help me, but you could – please, and then my baby can come with me." She moved toward the fireplace, staring sadly at Helen, her form fading and then disappearing.

Helen felt a falling sensation and then a jolt through her body that brought her into consciousness. *This is not going away. I am going to have to do something, and I think I know what it might be.* She was wide awake. She sat up in bed and looked around the moonlit room. The house was still. She sat for awhile pondering the words of the ghost. Suddenly, she had an idea, and smiled to herself. She determined that another trip to Crathes Castle would be required, and, with any luck, this would be the end of it. The only difficulty might be convincing the others to go along with the course of action she had just surmised was necessary. Instinctively she knew, somehow, what was the right thing to do and she hoped that the assistance she needed would be offered.

"Lenny, are you awake?" Sarah whispered as she opened the door to Helen's room. "I thought I heard something and wondered if you were up."

"Oh Sari, did I wake you? I am so sorry," Helen apologized, feeling terrible that she had disturbed anyone.

"I had another dream. She was here, or, at least in my dream. It was so vivid Sari, but I know what she wants now."

"Are you alright, Lenny? You didn't wake me – I was checking on the baby because I thought I had heard her, but she was asleep. Then I thought I heard something from your room, that's all." Sarah sat on the edge of the bed and smoothed the covers around Helen.

"Yes, I'm okay. I was just thinking about my dream, and figuring out what to do. I think I know – at least I think I know what to try. But I will tell you about it in the morning, Sari. There is nothing to worry about. I feel quite calm, really. I think that I can go back to sleep now."

"Okay, sweetie – see you in the morning." Sarah got up and quietly closed the door as she left. Helen nestled back into her pillows and fell asleep thinking about what she had to do in the morning. Hopefully she could enlist some help. *Let me just get this over with and done.*

Helen woke up early and ventured downstairs. She hoped that she could catch Ian before he left for the university to discuss what she had in mind. Ordinarily, he wouldn't be going out on a Sunday, but he had to meet with some colleagues about some administrative matters. Helen wasn't sure how he would react to her suggestion, but she felt in her gut that she was right in her thinking. Ian was alone in the kitchen having coffee and waiting for his oatmeal to cook. He looked surprised to see her.

"Good morning, Helen. You are up bright and early today. I thought you might take it easy today, especially after our experience yesterday. Would you like some coffee?" Helen nodded and smiled, sitting down at the table while Ian brought over a cup and poured the coffee.

"Thank you. I was awake and I wanted to catch you before you left today because I have a favour to ask of you." Ian dished up his oatmeal and sat down.

"Of course, Helen. What can I do?" he offered.

"Well, I had either another dream or another visit last night, from our friend in the green dress. I managed to remember what Matty had said about Geordie's advice to ask questions if I ever saw her again. Well, I did ask her what she wanted me to do. And she told me." Ian stopped eating his porridge and looked at her.

"What did she tell you?"

"She wants her baby blessed. I get the feeling that, for some reason, she has not 'crossed over' as they say because she is afraid that she will be leaving her baby, or parted from her baby somehow – if the baby is not blessed." Ian was looking skeptical. "I know it sounds crazy, and I am not sure what she means by that myself," stammered Helen, "but I know who to ask. I realized it last night."

"Who?" asked Ian.

"Reverend McDougall. I feel that she will know what to do. I am hoping she will help me."

Ian nearly choked on his oatmeal, coughed and then laughed. He tried to stifle himself but couldn't help it. He could just imagine the reaction of the Reverend. At first, Helen was annoyed that he was laughing, but, having met the Reverend, started to giggle herself.

"I'm sorry, Helen," he choked out, "the thought of us telling her about the ghost is just too funny." He was glad and relieved to see Helen was laughing too.

"I know, I know" said Helen, gasping by this time. She hadn't giggled like this in ages. Tears were running down her cheeks. She couldn't stop.

"What's so funny?" exclaimed Sarah, entering the room with little Helen on one hip. "I could hear you from the top of the stairs."

She never thought that she would see the day when Ian and Helen could be sharing a laugh. They were both always so serious, and kind of awkward when it came to humour. It made her smile to see them like this. Helen explained while she got Sarah some coffee, and Ian readied the baby's bottle and prepared some cereal for her.

"I think we should do it," stated Sarah, chuckling at the thought. "Seriously though, I think Helen is right. She will know what we should do, if anything at all."

"Aye, I suppose she will." Ian had regained control of himself and saw some merit in this suggestion. Reverend McDougall would either guide them further, or shut it down once and for all. It would be black or white. "She will be in her office this afternoon; she always is on Sunday afternoons – we could stop by to see her. I will call in on my way this morning to see if she could meet with us around three – would that suit?"

"Yes, that would be great. Thanks, Ian, so much," replied Helen, really grateful that he was willing to do this.

"Thank you, darling. You are a gem. We'll meet you there. When Matty gets up, we'll tell him the plan."

Sarah was pleased that, despite misgivings and the potential for possibly being viewed as insane, Ian was going to approach the Reverend on their behalf. She kissed him at the door as he left. It was a strange situation, but regardless, she was feeling pleased that, for the first time, Helen and Ian seemed to have found common ground.

Chapter 12 – Reverend MacDougall

There were not many at service this Sunday morning, the good Reverend noted with a sigh to herself as she carefully recorded her thoughts in her diary – something she did every day, but most particularly after a sermon. She found it useful for future reference as she composed her sermons. Often a thought or theme would arise during the service or as she spoke with individual congregation members as they shook her hand afterwards. She was trying very hard these days to make her sermons relevant to the daily lives of her dwindling congregation, knowing that the younger generations of the local families were not attending on a regular basis, if at all. Certainly the numbers increased significantly at Christmas and Easter, but as the elderly, devoted members of her church were passing away, there were fewer and fewer in attendance on Sundays. It was also becoming more difficult to find enough volunteers to keep the church activities and events going. Thank goodness there was still interest in having a choir and Sunday school. The Reverend herself had become actively involved in most activities out of necessity. In order for any special events to occur, all hands on deck were required. So, it was herself, the choir leader and the dwindling number of church elders who took on the organization and delivery of church events. Her church was not alone in this dilemma; most were struggling to figure out a new strategy for increasing membership and active participation.

Gladys Fionna MacDougall had known from a young age that she wanted to be a minister in her church. She had found comfort and a strong sense of belonging in the quiet order of attending church, the messages to be discovered in sermons and corresponding hymns, and the communion with fellow members as they participated in the ritual responses and exchanged greetings every Sunday. She had loved and been awe struck by the pageantry of the Christmas and Easter services, and, in general, felt at home and at peace within the particular architecture of her church with its stone arches, intricately carved vestry, and beautiful stained glass windows.

Her parents had been very involved in the church all of their lives, and she and her younger brother had been in regular attendance from the day they were baptized. When her brother became ill with polio at the age of seven, and died within a month, the Reverend and the church community had provided them with comfort and support as they grieved and came to terms with their loss. Gladys had been devastated by his death; they had done everything together and she had looked out for him as his older, by two years, sister. It was beyond her understanding how suddenly he was gone forever. Her parents, grief-stricken, had been rendered mute and could barely manage to get up and get dressed every day, let alone attend to daily routine. They continued on with work and household matters, but there was no joy in their eyes or actions for quite some time. However, the Reverend at the time was a daily presence, calling in to check on them and offer support and gentle encouragement to her parents, and to her. The ladies brought tasty meals to their home, and the men would quietly ensure that all was taken care of around their house and yard. Gladys noticed all of this and vowed to return the favour and blessing of this support by being as active herself within the community of her church.

As she grew older, took confirmation, and also embraced more responsible positions in the church, the Reverend and others took note that there was something special about her, that she had a gift for speaking and that her audience, whether it be a group of children in her Sunday school class, or a group of elders at a meeting, would listen intently – engaged in her words. She was encouraged to pursue her religious studies, and, with the support of her parents, she did and took her degree as the first step in her goal to becoming a leader in her church.

Getting the degree had been the easy part, finding a place as the head of a church had been more difficult, and had taken years. Twelve and some years of progressing through lower to more senior positions, supporting others in their career objectives, until finally, she was settled here as the Reverend. It had taken the Anglican leadership a long time to finally come to terms with having women as heads of congregations, but it was happening now, slowly, with more women moving into the upper ranks of the church. Gladys had had her own experiences of being passed over when she should have been the one to be given a leadership role, but she kept faith that her time would come, and it did, and she believed that, as a middle-aged woman, she had invaluable experience and, perhaps, more wisdom to offer her congregation. For that, she was grateful and believed fully that her path was destined to be what it was and what it had been.

So, here she was, on a Sunday afternoon, at her desk and thinking about how she could engender more interest in her church. She loved her office, with its grand oak desk and bookshelves, meticulously dusted and polished by the only employee of the church – old George, the caretaker. He lived there too, in a little room off the church kitchen, and had been resident and caretaker for forty years. It was his home and he cared for it lovingly and fiercely, and it glowed and shone with the fruits of his efforts. The grounds were trimmed and raked into perfection. Sunday was his only day off, and he was generally unseen after morning service. The elder ladies ensured that there was tea and coffee available after the eleven o'clock service for those who wished to stay, and, after they had cleaned up, they brought Reverend MacDougall a cold plate lunch and a pot of steaming tea. She looked forward to Sunday afternoons in her office as it was the one afternoon during the week where, after the others departed, she had solitude until she gave her shorter evening service at five o'clock.

A knock at her office door startled her out of her musings. As she crossed the stone floor to answer, she felt a little annoyed to be intruded upon unexpectedly. To her surprise, Ian Wallace stood before as she slowly opened the heavy carved door. She invited him inside, closed the door and offered him a cup of tea. Ian sat down in one of the leather chairs in front of her desk as she poured tea into a china cup, and then sat down in her chair on the other side.

"Well, this is a pleasant surprise, Mr. Wallace. I don't think I saw you this morning, did I?" They both knew that this was a rhetorical question and also the implication that went with it.

"No, Reverend, I'm sorry, I did not attend service this morning. I always think about it, but somehow, especially lately, with all the extra work and having company, ah, it's not happened as often as I would like." Ian stammered out, blushing as he spoke.

"That's unfortunate, indeed," she returned, "but I do understand how it is sometimes difficult to prioritize attending service into the demanding routine of work and family. I would encourage you to try though, you mind find it helpful. Now, if there is something I can do, please tell me."

She felt a bit sorry for sounding somewhat critical of his excuse; however, she attributed it to her frustration at the general lack of interest in the church amongst the younger generation. Although she wasn't that much older than Ian, she felt as if she belonged to a different generation altogether.

"Actually, Reverend, that's why I am here this afternoon," Ian replied, trying to get around the fact that they did not regularly attend church. "There is something I want to discuss with you, and to see if, perhaps, you can help me – us. It's a bit of an odd situation though – you may think it completely insane, but we need some guidance from someone who may, you know, who may know more about a situation like this than we do – as laypersons…" Ian was struggling with coming to his point.

"My goodness, Mr. Wallace, I am intrigued. Of course, if I can be of assistance, I will try my best. I am not here to judge, please continue." She sat back in her chair so as to seem more relaxed.

"Please call me Ian, Reverend," continued Ian, "And - well, in fact, you've met our friend Helen Brooks, and it's a matter that concerns her, and us. If possible, Helen and my wife, Sarah, would like to be here to discuss the situation too. Would we be able to see you together in an hour or so? We won't take up too much of your time."

"I do have my service at five o'clock, but if you come back at two thirty, I can spend an hour or so with you. Can you give me some indication of the nature of your situation" she asked.

"Yes, well," stammered Ian, "the nature of it is the difficult part. You see, it has to do with spirits, a particular spirit, and some experiences that Helen has been having since she arrived a couple of weeks ago. I know it sounds ridiculous, Reverend, but we need some assistance or someone to talk to and, Helen, actually it was her idea, thought that we should approach you for advice." *Whew. There it was.* Ian waited for Reverend MacDougall's response nervously.

"Oh. I see. Very intriguing. Well, I shall see you all at two thirty, then, and, in the meantime, I will give it a little thought. Relax, Ian, this is not the first time that someone has asked me about matters of this nature. It seems that there is a very active spiritual world in Scotland – yes indeed – it is well documented! Let's meet then and talk, and see what we can do. Now, if you will excuse me, I must finish something before we meet again later."

The Reverend ushered Ian out the door, and returned to her seat. This was certainly an interesting state of affairs. She wondered what could possibly have been happening to Helen Brooks. She stifled her curiosity in order to attend to matters at hand. She must put the finishing touches on her evening service. It looked like this would be a different kind of Sunday afternoon for her. She felt a twinge of excitement at the prospect of something outside of her usual routine.

Ian was surprised by Reverend MacDougall's response at first, but then, as she had pointed out, the topic of spirits was not foreign to anyone in Scotland. Many believed in ghosts and many did not. He would have included himself in the latter category until his own recent experience. He remembered that many years ago, when they were still children, after their mother died of cancer, Matt had told him he felt his mother's presence one night. He hadn't said too much at the time because Matt had seemed happier as a result, than he had been in the weeks since she had died. But he had not believed it himself, and attributed it to Matt's young imagination combined with his grief over losing his precious mummy. Anyway, Ian was relieved that the good Reverend had agreed to speak with them, and to help in any way that she could. He called Sarah with the news and they agreed to meet later at the church.

Chapter 13– An Unusual Request

Ian was waiting for them when they pulled into the parking area at the church. Helen and Sarah had not spoken much since the morning. They had both been preoccupied with their own thoughts about what to say to Reverend MacDougall. Matt had been unable to come with them, as he had received a call from a gallery in Edinburgh with an urgent request for him to come to meet with an art dealer visiting from Dubai. Matt thought that the plan to ask Reverend MacDougall for guidance was a good idea, although, he was unsure about how receptive she would be to their proposal. He wasn't sure how long he would have to stay in Edinburgh, but probably overnight at least.

Matt had already left when Ian had called with the news, so Sarah and Helen decided to wait until evening to call him with the results of the meeting. Helen was disappointed that he had to leave, but Ian's reaction to it all had provided her with enough of a sense of support to go through with this discussion. Nonetheless, she was nervous about the meeting; it was very uncomfortable for her to be in a situation that she felt she had little control over. Sarah was confident that they were on the right path, and that whatever the Reverend determined was required, they would do it and move on. She did not like to see her friend worried or anxious about things; it reminded her of how timid and unsure of herself Helen was as a little girl, in contrast with the confident, brilliant professional she had become over the years.

When Ian arrived at the church, the girls were already there waiting for him.

"Hi Ian," Helen greeted him, stepping out of the car. "Thank you for setting this up. I hope she can help."

Sarah unbuckled the baby from her car seat, and handed her to Ian. He snuggled the little girl, and she grabbed the end of his nose with her tiny hand. Helen smiled and felt such love for them all. *I am so fortunate to be a part of this family.* Tears came to her eyes as she thought about the love and protection that little Sarah Helen had from all of them. Something within her stirred and she thought also, with sadness, about the poor ghost lady and her baby. *Whatever had happened to them?*

"Lenny, are you okay?" Sarah gently took Helen's hand as they opened the door to the church. "We are here for you, don't worry. Whatever she says, we'll do it. I feel sure that she will know. Your instincts are good." Helen smiled gratefully at Sarah and squeezed her hand.

"I'm fine, Sari, really. I am prepared to follow her advice." They walked down the hall to the Reverend's office door, and Ian knocked as the three exchanged a look of some trepidation.

"Good afternoon, Mr. and Mrs. Wallace and Miss Brooks, come in won't you? Thank you for being punctual," said the Reverend as she swung open the heavy door. "Have a seat please. How is the wee bairn, oh, she's a bonnie lass, my word. The good Lord has blessed the dear little one."

Reverend MacDougall closed the door and took her seat behind her desk, and leaned forward, clasping her hands together in front of her. She could see that they were nervous, and she looked directly at each one of them as she spoke.

"Now, Mr. Wallace – Ian – told me a tiny bit about what's happened, and why you wanted to see me. Miss Brooks, I don't want you to feel uncomfortable about giving me some details about what has transpired. As I mentioned to Ian earlier today, yours is not the first experience of this nature that I have been consulted about, nor will it, I imagine, be the last one." With that, she looked squarely at Helen, and leaned back in her chair waiting.

"Thank you, Reverend MacDougall, I surely appreciate you saying that. I really feel uncomfortable with this whole situation, however, I also feel compelled to do something about it. I am not sure why I cannot just ignore it – it's a feeling I cannot rationally explain," remarked Helen.

As she spoke, she noticed a sensation of weight bearing down upon her shoulders. Her voice trembled slightly as she told the Reverend about her first dream, and then about the trip to Crathes, and the experience she had in the nursery there. She continued, in obvious discomfort, describing the second trip to Crathes, and then about the details of the dream she had had since then. She felt a chilly sensation and shivered as she recounted her experiences. Sarah noticed her distress, and helped by mentioning the day they had spent in town trying to do some research about the Crathes ghost lady, expressing her irritation at the reception Helen had received from the staff at the National Trust office. Reverend MacDougall listened intently to everything, and seemed intrigued when Ian interjected to tell her that he, too, had seen something in the Crathes nursery. When Helen was finally finished, she slumped down into her chair, exhausted, and stared down at her lap.

"Well – this is very interesting, indeed," the Reverend noted quietly, and she leaned forward to pick up her pen. "Certainly, as you have been made aware by our friendly local National Trust representatives, others have also seen ghosts in many of our castles and ancient landmarks. So, Dr. Brooks, I hope that you will not feel embarrassed about your experience, especially because, as you have pointed out, you are a scientist and this is entirely out of your realm of experience. Many others – professionals of all sorts and laypersons alike, have had these experiences across our great country. So please be at ease about that point," she nodded at Helen and smiled to see the relief in the poor woman's eyes. "Now, I would like to know what, in particular, do you think I could help you with in this matter, and then I will be able to tell you what is possible or not."

Helen sat upright and mustered the most confident tone she could, having been bolstered by the Reverend's reassurances.

"Please call me Helen, Reverend. The idea I have came to me after my last dream, and encounter with it – the ghost. I don't know if you could – if it would be possible, but I feel instinctively that what I am going to propose may be the right thing to do."

"Go on, Helen, what is your idea?" The Reverend leaned forward looking intently at Helen.

"I think that if, somehow, we – us – with you – could go to Crathes, to the nursery, and baptize the resting place of the baby – where the bones were found – perhaps the mother and the baby could - you know – go to where they should be - into the light or whatever, and, hopefully, be at peace." Helen mumbled this out, feeling really uncomfortable with the nature of what she was saying, and even more worried about the Reverend's reaction to her idea. "I have the utmost respect for you and your profession, Reverend, and I hope you don't think I am being disrespectful by asking you to do this."

"Thank you, Helen, I appreciate your concern. Rest assured that I do not think any such thing. Strangely, perhaps, and perhaps peculiarly, I do not think that my responsibility for the souls of my congregation ends at their deaths. And that is because for those they leave behind, there is always a need for care and attention from me in some form or another." She paused for a few minutes and looked down at her notes.

"Now, in this situation, the departed have been gone for well over a century and more; however, for whatever reason, their souls have found an audience in yourself and, to some extent, Ian. As a member of my congregation, perhaps not as active a member as I would wish, but a member nonetheless, Ian," she looked directly at him as he squirmed in his chair, "I feel it is my responsibility to help you as much as I can in this matter." The Reverend paused again, and looked down at her notes for a moment, then at Helen.

"I think that there is some merit in your idea, and I am willing to help by performing a baptismal blessing. I will have to adapt it for the situation, obviously – we are not dealing with a normal baptism here. Nevertheless, I could do something that will suffice for the purpose. That being said, I am not sure that those in charge at Crathes will be as receptive to your wishes. I do not see any harm in it myself; however, I cannot be a part of anything that I know is not approved by those responsible for the care of the castle. So, here is what I would be prepared to do. If you can find a way to do this, with the agreement of a Crathes representative, I will be pleased to perform a blessing at the site of where the bones were found in the nursery. I believe that this will satisfy the needs of the ghosts, mother and child and, hopefully, send them on their way; and, more importantly, provide you and the Wallace family with some peace. Does that sound fair, Helen – Ian – and Sarah?" She sat back in her chair and looked at each of them, somewhat amused at the surprised looks on their faces at her response.

"Yes, of course – thank you so much, Reverend. I am so relieved and, frankly, pleasantly surprised that you will do this. Thank you." Helen brightened visibly and felt the weight lift off of her shoulders.

"You are welcome, my dear. But you must wait to see what kind of cooperation, if any, you will get from Crathes. I am not sure that it will be possible."

Reverend MacDougall got up from her chair and came around the desk toward the door.

"Now, I really must get ready for evening service. Thank you for coming, and please let me know how things go with the folks at Crathes. Once I know, I can prepare myself accordingly."

Ian picked up the baby who had fallen asleep in her car seat, and Sarah and Helen followed him out the door, thanking the Reverend for her time and extraordinary offer of help to them. They continued out to the parking lot and stared at each other, incredulous about what had just transpired.

"I never thought she would so readily agree to something like this, I have to admit," Ian murmured to them, shaking his head. "She really does not fit the mold of the type of minister that I grew up with here. Matt will be quite surprised to hear about her reaction to it all."

Helen took the baby and buckled her in, and sat beside her feeling more relaxed than she had for a long time. Sarah got in and the three rode in silence for the short distance to the house, with Ian following behind in his car. As they pulled into the yard, the boys ran up to greet them, begging Helen and Ian to play football with them for awhile. Sarah took the baby and began preparations for dinner while the others had a rigorous game of footy on the lawn. She laughed as she watched them through the large windows of the kitchen, grateful that the meeting and Crathes events could be forgotten if even for a little while.

Chapter 14 - Permission to Proceed

Ian retreated immediately into his study when Sarah called the boys to come in for dinner, and placed a call to Matt to tell him the good news. Matt had just finished his meeting with the dealer from Saudi Arabia, but had to stay overnight in Edinburgh so that he could complete the purchase and shipping arrangements for a number of his paintings as soon as business opened on Monday morning. He suggested to Ian that they meet at Crathes at two in the afternoon to discuss the desired plan with the National Trust site manager, Geordie, who had been very sympathetic to Helen's experience at the castle. As Ian had predicted, Matt was astonished that Reverend MacDougall had agreed to perform a blessing in the nursery at Crathes. Matt had envisioned them receiving a hearty dressing-down from her about spending time on such things as ghosts, let alone planning to have a deliberate interaction with them. The thought of her probable reaction had provided some amusement; however, he was quickly sobered by the reality of the distress it was causing Helen. It was going to be very interesting to see what transpired next, if anything. Matt was optimistic, though, because of Geordie's own and others' experiences in the castle and the fact that he had made some concrete suggestions about what Helen should do and say if and when she next encountered the spirit. Besides, she had followed Geordie's advice about asking the ghost what it wanted, and surmised a plan as a result. Hopefully, Geordie would now also agree to help with its execution!

Helen and Sarah busied themselves with the children's dinner while Ian spoke with Matt. Betty had baked some of her savoury meatpies before the weekend, so Sarah had warned them in the Aga and made a salad with fresh greens from the garden. The boys had played at a friend's home for the afternoon and gobbled up their meals with great enthusiasm. They loved Betty's cooking. Helen fed the baby while Sarah set the table for the three of them to have their dinner later.

Ian joined them after the children were bathed and in bed. Sarah greeted him with a glass of wine and a hug. Despite the unusual circumstances, Ian felt content as he sat down at the table and smiled at his dining companions, filling them in on what Matt had suggested they do.

"I have classes and a faculty meeting tomorrow afternoon, Helen, so I cannot be with you. Sarah, will you be able to take Helen? I am not sure how comfortable she is with driving on the left side."

"I hate to be so much trouble you two." Helen said, nodding in agreement. "But I am petrified of driving on the wrong side of the road. If you could drop me off at the castle, Sari, Matt can bring me home. Would that be all right?"

"Of course it would." Sarah said firmly and smiled, "and it is no trouble. We're all in this together. But that will work out well for me too. Betty is here tomorrow so I can leave the baby with her for a short while and then be back in time to do some things around here that need doing, and be here when the boys get home too."

"Thanks." Helen looked relieved. "The sooner we can determine if this is going to work, or not, the better. If Geordie agrees to our plan, Matt and I can set up the time with him and confirm it with the Reverend. Hopefully, we can do this very soon. Like this week sometime. I can't believe how quickly the time is passing. I will be going home in less than two weeks!" She accepted another glass of wine from Ian, and followed him and Sarah to sit by the fireplace. "I am going to miss this place and being with you. You have such a wonderful home and family. You are so fortunate, and I am fortunate to be a part of it for awhile."

"Aye, Helen, we are fortunate, indeed. Especially me," replied Ian as he put his arm around Sarah and hugged her. "And you are welcome here anytime that you can come. It is a pleasure to have you. The children love you. You are family."

Ian was sincere in his sentiments; Helen and Sarah looked at each other and smiled. This was a change for the better. After all these years. Was this just a product of maturity? Or was it a result of his peculiar circumstance that they had been thrust into? Whatever the reason, all three parties were happy that a peaceful relationship seemed to be on the horizon.

The next day, when Sarah dropped Helen at Crathes, Geordie Macgillvary was standing outside the visitor's entrance smoking a cigarette. He stubbed it out when he saw Helen, and walked toward her, offering his hand.

"Good day, ma'am; Dr. Brooks – am I correct?"

"Yes, how are you? And it's Helen, please," returned Helen, smiling at him as Sarah drove away. "Has Matthew arrived yet?"

"No, he has not, but he did call me this morning just before he left Edinburgh to say that you were coming and why. He should be here any moment. Would you like to come in and wait in my office? May I offer you a cup of tea? Or coffee?"

Geordie led Helen through the entrance and to his office. She stated her preference and settled herself in a chair while he went out to fetch some tea from the kitchen. Almost as soon as she entered the building, she began to feel a pressure on her shoulders – just as she had on the previous visits. She looked around his office nervously, but there was nothing unusual there. It was a pleasant, peaceful sort of room with three tall and narrow windows. He had a beautiful old mahogany table that he used for a desk. It was somewhat cluttered with various items – small statues and vases, some inkwells and a number of old fashioned fountain pens. Helen admired the bookcases that lined the stone walls, filled with neatly placed hardcovers that appeared to be first editions. Geordie came back with some steaming cups of tea and offered one to Helen, and she took it from him, grateful for the warmth of the cup in her hands as she felt chilly despite having worn a thick sweater.

"Thank you, Geordie, you are very thoughtful. I don't know why but I have never been so cold in my life as I have been since I've been in Scotland," she mused, sipping her tea.

"Aye, Helen, you are not the first person to tell me that, oh no, many feel the chill – I expect it's the wind and the high humidity combined that give our visitors the willies. It's a great boon to our sweater industry though," he smiled at her across the desk. "Now, Helen, I gather from Mathew that the Reverend MacDougall from Aberdeenshire is willing to conduct a sort of baptismal blessing in our nursery here at Crathes if the site management will sanction it."

"Yes, Geordie, she has – much to our surprise. She was not entirely optimistic that the National Trust would agree to such an activity, however…." Helen looked at him with some trepidation in anticipation of his answer. "What do you think, Geordie? Will we be able to get permission?"

"I have been thinking about this since Mathew called this morning. Technically, I am the site manager here for the National Trust; so, in my own opinion, I could make the call. I consulted the site management guidelines and my interpretation of the policy around hosting events on the grounds leads me to believe that there is no reason for me to consult our regional office. For example, we have allowed wedding ceremonies to take place on the grounds, as well as some charitable events, with the only permission required of the site manager – myself – in these cases. I think that what you and Mathew are proposing is along these lines; therefore, I have no opposition to your conducting this event on the premises. And if," he said, with a slight smile and a wink, "…in fact, it turns out afterwards that I was wrong in the eyes of the National Trust, I will apologize to them for my mistake."

Geordie noticed that Helen looked relieved as he explained his thinking on the matter. "I do think, however, that perhaps we may approach the event slightly differently from others, given the nature of some of the proposed participants."

He looked at his watch and back at Helen. "Mr. Wallace should be here momentarily, so I suggest that we wait to discuss the details." Helen nodded in agreement and sipped her tea, and they talked about her visit to Scotland in generalities until Matthew arrived.

Matthew had taken care of his business requirements first thing that morning, but it had taken somewhat longer than he anticipated. Knowing that Helen would be at Crathes by herself concerned him a little, and he hoped that she and Geordie would not decide to go up to the nursery without him – just in case she had another ghostly encounter. Geordie seemed like a trustworthy sort of fellow, not only possessed with a lot of common sense, but also enough imagination to be open to what was going on and not assume that they had 'lost the plot'. Because Geordie had quite readily discussed Helen's encounter with the ghost in the nursery, Matthew felt sure that he was the requisite 'official' to facilitate their plan. An historian and curator by profession, Geordie had also sensed the existence of spirits in the castle and had not been alarmed. Rather, he had an expectation of them in Scotland's carefully protected historic sites, given the many documented cases of those who had experienced their presence. Matthew, like most Scots, was well aware of the ghost stories associated with Scotland's historic and other places. They were as much a part of Scottish history and lore as the famous battles and the birthplace of great royal families. As he drove into the parking area at Crathes, he felt a combination of excitement and trepidation. He could certainly understand why Helen felt that, on some level, all of this was quite ridiculous, however compelled she also felt that something concrete must be done about it. As intelligent professionals, it just didn't make sense and seemed outrageous that they could be involved in such an adventure. On the other hand, there were the dreams and the uncanny coincidence of her experience that could not be ignored. Someday, they would look back on it all and probably shake their heads at what they had gotten up to. For now, they would pursue it and hope for a resolution.

"Hello, Helen. Mr. Macgillvary, great to see you again and thanks for making yourself available to us this afternoon. I am sorry that I'm a bit later than I thought I would be. The postal bureaucracy is the bane of my existence these days!"

Matthew, ushered into Geordie's office, sat down in the chair next to Helen, briefly resting his hand reassuringly on her shoulder. He was relieved to see them both in the office and, moreso, to see that Helen looked relaxed and comfortable. For her part, Helen felt happier and a sense of contentment when Matthew arrived, and the touch of his hand on her shoulder provided more to her than friendly reassurance, much to her surprise. She had the unfamiliar sense suddenly that she was not alone in the most profound sense of belonging. No matter how many people were around, she had always felt alone. She could not remember ever having felt otherwise. Except when she was with Sarah. And now, it seemed, with Matthew. Although it was somewhat different than the sense of sisterly kindred spirit that she felt when she was with Sarah. With Matthew, there was also a twinge of excitement, precipitated by this touch of his hand. It was only a fleeting few seconds of contact that caused Helen this sensation, as she looked at him and smiled.

"Aye, no worries, Mr. Wallace, as you can imagine, we have had our own encounters with that bastion of efficiency. Please call me Geordie, sir, it makes me uncomfortable to be called by Mr. – that's reserved for my good father, so it is." Geordie leaned over to shake Matthew's hand across the desk.

"Aye, I'd be delighted, thank you, Geordie. The same goes for me as well. When someone calls me Mr. Wallace, I think that I am in trouble," laughed Matthew. "Well now, have you two had a chance to discuss our wee plan?" He looked at the two of them, and they both nodded.

"Yes, as I have been telling Helen, after your call this morning, I had some time to think about how it could be approached."

Geordie explained his rationale for facilitating their plan as he had done so with Helen. Matthew was pleased to hear it, albeit somewhat surprised to hear that permission would be achieved so easily.

"I would suggest one slight difference from some other events that we have had here. I think that it might be wise to have it either very early in the morning or in the early evening – 7 am or 7 pm to be precise, and either before or after my staff arrives in the morning or leaves in the evening. I will explain why," continued Geordie, as he stood up and walked over to close his office door. " I will, of course, be here, but I would prefer that we keep our plans confidential, and not involve any others of the castle's staff. This is for a couple of reasons. Some may be fearful, as there are many who are afraid of the presence of ghosts, despite working here. And, secondly, the "green lady ghost" is, if you will, a resident of the castle, and some might be upset at the prospect that she may be leaving for good." He looked at them to gauge their reaction.

"Geordie, we'll comply with whatever arrangements you think best – of course." Matt replied. "We will have to propose the options to Reverend MacDougall and defer to her preference. What do you think, Helen?"

"I absolutely agree, and, thank you again Geordie. I am so relieved and grateful that you will help me – us. Thank you."

Helen stifled a sob and was surprised at herself showing emotion. Obviously, she had underestimated the stress that this had caused her. She could only hope that she hadn't caused the others this degree of consternation. It couldn't be helped, however, she had to do something and this was it. Now that they had both the Reverend and Geordie on side, she was anxious to put the plan in motion.

Matt thanked Geordie for his understanding and willingness to facilitate their request. He knew that Helen had been upset, but hadn't realized quite how much. He helped her from the chair and put his arm around her as they said their goodbyes and left. It was a silent walk to the car, with the exception of the gravel crunching under their feet. Matt opened the car door for Helen and walked to his side. As he backed out of his spot, Helen looked up at the nursery window. To her astonishment, a woman's face was visible in the window, and it was looking right back down at her. Helen gasped and looked away. When she took a glance back as they drove down the lane, the face was gone.

"What is it, Lenny?" ask Matt, concerned at the look on her face.

"I saw her in the nursery window. She looked right at me. It felt like she was looking through me." Helen shivered and pulled her sweater closer to her.

"Probably she is one of the staff, Lenny, don't you think?"

"You're right. Probably was." muttered Helen. "I'm falling apart. I have to get it together."

"No worries. I'm going to get Ian to call Reverend MacDougall as soon as we get to the house. I'll call him at the office if he's not at home. Let's get this done as soon as we can."

Matt was beginning to worry that the entire business was taking too much of a toll on Helen. It was time to take definitive action. Geordie was ready. All they had to do was get the Reverend to choose a day and time within his parameters.

"Don't worry Lenny," said Matt, reaching over to take one of her hands, "this will all be over soon." Helen felt reassured and calmed down, and squeezed his hand in acknowledgement.

"Thank you so much, Matt, you've been wonderful. You all have. Especially you. I can't tell you how much this means to me."

"It's really my pleasure, Helen. It's been so great to spend time with you. You are not like anyone else I have ever met. I hope that once we get this behind us, we can spend some time together before you leave." He paused. "Actually, I have something to ask you, but I don't want to put any additional pressure on you right now." He glanced over to see her reaction, and was encouraged to see her smiling back at him.

"What is it, Matt, please. If there is something, anything that I can do for you, I would be happy to."

"Well, I think I mentioned that I had met recently with some people from New York who liked my paintings. They called me yesterday and asked if I would consider having a show at the gallery owned by a friend of theirs in Manhattan. I agreed to do it – the catch is, it's in three weeks. I was thinking that maybe I could fly back to Toronto with you – there are also a few art dealers there who have been wanting to meet with me. I could spend a few days there, and then go to New York. I would love it if you would consider coming with me to Manhattan as well." He looked over at Helen, hoping that he was not overwhelming her with his idea.

"Of course, by all means you are welcome to stay with me in Toronto, and I would love to have the company on the flight home," Helen said softly. "I have to warn you though, I have a fear of flying so I am not the best company." She laughed suddenly.

"When am I good company, for heaven's sake? Frankly, I am astonished that you want to spend more time with me, Matt, you must be nuts!"

Matt laughed and then slowly eased the car over to the side of the road and stopped. He turned and looked at Helen. "I don't think that I'm crazy, Lenny, but I do have feelings for you, Lenny. I mean – more that friendship type of feelings. Let me put it this way, there is nobody else that I am more eager to spend time with right now."

Helen felt a blush creeping to her cheeks and looked down at her hands. "I am very fond of you too, Matt. It's a new experience for me, despite my age, but I feel something for you too, and I would love to spend more time with you. The thought of it makes me happy."

She looked up at him, and as their gaze met, they both knew immediately that this was definitely more than friendship. A kiss sealed this acknowledgement of their mutual affection, and they sat in an embrace for awhile longer, oblivious to the cars whizzing by them.

Sarah was watching out the kitchen window for Matt's car as she gave the children their dinner, anxious for Matt and Helen to get home. She hoped that everything would work out according to their plan, and was eager to put it into action. With Betty there for most of the day to watch the baby, she had also had time to locate and begin to unpack the boxes containing her thesis research. As she browsed through her findings, it became clear to her that she must continue. A number of discoveries and advances had been achieved in breast cancer research during the hiatus from her own studies; however, her focus at the time was on a potential early intervention that had yet to manifest. Her interest was rekindled, and she decided then and there that she would talk to Ian about restarting her work. The logistics of where and how would have to be worked out, but she determined that minimal disruption to her family would be a priority. This meant that she would have to see if Aberdeen University would accept her as a transfer PhD student and give her credit for her courses and thesis work thus far. It was a stretch, but they might do it. Nothing ventured, nothing gained, and she believed that following her research to its conclusions might contribute in a meaningful way to finding better early interventional treatment for those at highest risk for breast cancer. Helen would be so pleased to hear about her decision. She hoped that Ian, if not thrilled, would, at least, be supportive.

Ian's car pulled into the drive and he gave her a wave when he saw her in the kitchen window. She smiled and waved back at him, watching as he reached into the rear seat of the car for his briefcase. She was relieved and pleased to have him home earlier than usual, especially since she had been on pins and needles wondering what had transpired at Crathes since dropping Helen off there.

"Hello my love. How was your day? Hello boys and girl!" Ian bent over to kiss the baby, and ruffled the boys' hair as he strode over to kiss Sarah.

"Productive, darling, amazingly productive." Sarah smiled up at him and patted his cheek affectionately. "I have some news, and a favour to ask you – later though. I am dying to hear what happened at Crathes today – I thought that they would be back by now."

"Me too – that's partly why I left earlier than usual today. I hope it went well, and we can actually to this thing." Ian looked at her intently, and then smiled. "But I am intrigued that you have a 'favour' to ask me. It must be something major or you would just give me an order. You have got my curiosity going now, dear one!"

Sarah laughed. "You will just have to be patient. In the meantime, speaking of ordering you about, could you get the children washed up? And maybe check the boys' homework over with them?"

"Certainly I can. Come boys, and little girl. Let's go clean up, and if we get everything Mummy wants done, maybe we can read or something." Ian took little Helen and the boys eagerly jumped to their feet, thrilled that their Daddy was home early.

"Thank you darling. I will tidy-up here and get our dinner ready for when the others get home." Sarah busily loaded the dishwasher and wiped the table. She had set the dining room earlier, and checked on the baked ribs she was cooking for their dinner. Everything was ready except for the salad, so she prepared her dressing and began chopping tomatoes and onions. Ribs and Greek salad was one of Ian's favourite dinners. As she worked away, she thought about what she would say to him later. Hopefully, they would get a chance to talk about her academic plans.

Helen and Matt drove the rest of the way without much conversation. They were each contemplating their respective feelings for each other, along with the prospect of spending more time together – just the two of them. This, accompanied by the glorious sensations of new love and attraction for each other superseded a need for conversation. When they arrived at the house, they were greeted by the wonderful aroma of dinner, and a smiling Sarah who was obviously pleased to see them. After they had freshened up, they went downstairs to find Ian and Sarah having a glass of wine, while the boys entertained their baby sister as she lay on a blanket, rolling over and smiling at them as they cheered her on.

"Well – don't keep us in suspense! What did Geordie say? Do we have a green light for the green ghost plan?" Ian bombarded them as he poured a glass of wine for each.

"Aye brother, it's a green light indeed. Just one minor hurdle to jump and we are in business," responded Matt, glancing at Helen to see if Ian's jocular approach had bothered her.

"Yes, Ian. We can proceed with it," added Helen, resigned to Ian's awkward sense of humour. "Geordie is fantastic and very understanding. He will facilitate everything himself. We just have to confirm the day and time. He has given us two options, and I thought that Reverend MacDougall should select the one that suits her best. That is, if you and Sarah agree, of course."

Helen looked over at Matt who took over and explained what Geordie had suggested to them and why. Ian offered to make the call the following morning to the Reverend with the news, and Matt suggested that he would immediately confirm with Geordie once they knew her preference. Once this was settled, Matt also shared his proposed travel to North America. Helen noticed Sarah's raised eyebrows and subsequent grin when Matt mentioned that they had tentative plans to travel together when Helen returned to Canada. She and Sarah exchanged a look, a knowing look, and she could see that Sarah was pleased with this new development. Ian looked rather startled as Matt announced his intentions, but quickly composed his expression as he listened. Matt picked up on this and felt a pang as he thought that he should probably have told Ian in private first. He suspected that Ian would surmise that this was just another whim of his and that, once again, he would not be around much, despite his previous recent declarations to the contrary. It also did not immediately occur to Ian that there was more to the travel plan than connecting with some interested art buyers.

Sarah was indeed pleased and was anxious to hear more about it from Helen when they were next alone. However, as they continued to talk late into the evening, it became apparent that her own news would have to wait for another day. It was too late and they were all too tired to launch into the topic of the resurrection of her research. She would have to try to talk to Ian in the morning before he left for work. To be fair to him, she wanted to be sure of his support and agreement before she shared news of her decision with anyone – even Helen.

Chapter 15 – The Plan is Set in Motion

As was her habit, Reverend MacDougall was at her desk in the rectory office by seven o'clock in the morning, having already taken a brisk walk, followed by a steaming cup of tea and a breakfast of toast and jam. She enjoyed the solitude of early morning before the church secretary arrived at nine. From then on, it seemed, there was a steady stream of activity – mostly administrative. So, she was somewhat surprised when the phone rang at eight, and it was Ian Wallace with the news that the baptism at Crathes castle could take place. She suggested that he drop by her office later in the afternoon on his way home and that, by then, she would have determined which option presented to her suited her best. She wanted some time to think about how she would approach this unusual ceremony, and also to consult some particular texts in her library for guidance. It must be performed with seriousness and solemnity. If it would assist some poor lost souls to achieve peace, then what could be the harm in it? Some colleagues might think her mad for agreeing to it, but she felt it was her duty to support her parishioners in their time of need – however unique or challenging.

Ian pulled into the church parking lot just as old Gregor was packing up his tools for the day. He had raked the gravel into perfect lines and frowned as Ian's car disturbed the even surface of the driveway and parking area. The hedges were freshly clipped and the flowered borders provided a bright contrast to the grey of the gravel and stone of the church. Ian admired the orderliness of it as he exited his car and strode toward the entrance.

"Good afternoon, sir," he said to Gregor, "I say my good man, you do a marvelous job of keeping these grounds."

He nodded appreciatively at the old man. Gregor looked at him suspiciously and grunted.

"Aye, sir. It would be a might easier if people were more considerate and did'na trample the place and leave their litter about."

Ian chuckled to himself and smiled at the old man, despite the fact that it was obvious Gregor did not particularly like to see anyone disturb his neatly executed work. *The old curmudgeon – he will never change. He would be happier if there were no parishioners.*

Reverend MacDougall was in her office, having just finished reading the references she had wanted to look at in preparation for Ian's visit. The door was open and Ian timidly tapped at the door frame and entered the room.

"Excellent timing Mr. Wallace! I am ready for our discussion. Sit yourself down here and let me outline how I envision this peculiar event. I do not mean that in a pejorative manner, dear man, but it is a peculiar circumstance – from other baptisms. However, I have consulted for some guidance, and I believe that I have arrived at a methodology appropriate for our situation."

She was clearly excited, but business-like at the same time. This was a challenge that must be met, and she had determined a suitable solution that would not in any way compromise the sacredness and solemnity of the holy baptism.

"I am relieved and pleased to hear it," Ian said as he took a seat in front of her desk. "Frankly, I was concerned about that aspect of what we are planning to do." He paused and looked at her across the desk. She was reading some notes that she had made that afternoon. "When and how do you think we should proceed?"

"I suggest that we not waste any time in getting this done. It is my understanding that Miss Brookes leaves next week, so I think that we should tell Mr. MacGillvary that Friday morning at sunrise will be an excellent time. It is my particular opinion that this is best done in the morning. I always feel that with every sunrise comes a fresh start, with hope for best outcomes. The process will take about forty minutes from start to finish; the ceremony itself, about 10 minutes of that. We need the rest of the time to get set up for the ceremony, and then to pack up my items afterwards and leave Crathes by the time any of the staff arrive. What do you think? Can you be prepared by Friday?"

Ian nodded yes, and felt a nervous excitement in his stomach. It was really going to happen.

"Now for some particulars. I cannot perform the holy baptism proper for several reasons that are probably apparent to yourself. Firstly, the recipient is deceased and, secondly, there will be no 'godparents' who will be guiding the recipient or taking responsibility for the recipient's religious upbringing. This fact, notwithstanding, there are provisions for baptism of the deceased, for example, a stillborn child. In addition, there is provision for the blessing of a deceased person's soul and, in particular, for the blessing of a deceased baby. I believe that I can perform a hybrid of the holy baptism and a blessing, in order to satisfy our requirements. Hopefully, this will suffice to give the poor souls we are assisting some peace." The reverend sat back in her chair and looked at Ian for a response.

"Yes. Absolutely. It sounds reasonable, and I agree with your plan, Reverend. Thank you for taking the time to figure out how we can do this according to the tenets of the Church, and in a respectful manner. I agree that we must approach it with all due seriousness and solemnity, and ensure that this is not some frivolous exercise to appease a tourist with an overactive imagination. I saw what I saw there myself, so I know that Helen is not creating something out of nothing – not that she would be inclined to do so in the first place."

"Exactly my sentiments and, hence, approach, Ian. I know that all of you are on the same wavelength where this is concerned. As I have said before, this is not the first time that I have heard of such a thing, and it won't be the last. Although this 'blessing', and I do prefer to call it a 'blessing' because that is what is appropriate for the circumstances, this blessing will be a first of its kind for me." She smiled at Ian and rose to see him out. He responded to her cue, and made his way to the door.

"Thank you very much, Reverend MacDougall. I really appreciate this."

"You are welcome, Ian. I am pleased that I can be of assistance to you. I will meet you at Crathes at sunrise on Friday morning. Gregor will drive me. Good day, Ian, and please give my regards and blessing to the others. Do assure them that we will be allright, and do it justice."

With that, she escorted Ian outside and watched as he drove off. She would enlist Gregor's assistance to get ready for Friday and to drive her there and back. Within less than forty eight hours, the deed would be done.

Chapter 16 – Upon the Hearth a Blessing

The others were somewhat taken aback when Ian returned from his meeting with Reverend MacDougall and brought the news that the baptism would take place on Friday morning. Matt confirmed the time with Geordie MacGillvary immediately thereafter. Sarah suggested that Matt, Ian and Helen go without her, and she would remain at home with the children to keep a normal schedule. She briefly contemplated asking Betty to stay over Thursday to look after the children while she went with the others to Crathes. However, that would mean explaining the situation to Betty, and they all decided that it was unnecessary and perhaps unwise to enlighten any others as to what was going to transpire at the castle, or about the reasons behind it. As much as she wanted to be there to support Helen, Sarah felt confident that Matt and Ian would provide sufficient protection for her friend.

Early Friday morning, as they left the house in darkness, Helen looked back to wave at her friend.

"Don't worry, Sari" she called out softly, "it will be fine – we will be fine - back before you know it." Sarah waved back and nodded, trying to smile encouragingly at them.

"Poor Sarah," said Ian, "She really wanted to be with you, Lenny… mostly for protection purposes. She's a real mother bear when it comes to those she loves."

"I know, Ian. She will worry the whole time we are gone. I wish this was over with. I have to admit that my stomach is in knots."

"Aye, Lenny, I think we all are anxious. I hardly slept a wink," added Matt, looking over the seat at her as he drove. They continued the rest of the way in silence. The atmosphere in the car was heavy with a combination of dread and excitement. When they drove up to the castle, the sky was getting a bit lighter as dawn approached. Reverend MacDougall's car was already there, but there was no sign of her or old Gregor. Helen, Matt and Ian walked up to the entrance and pushed open the heavy door. There was nobody in the hall. Ian closed the door and walked over to Geordie's office. He looked in and saw that Geordie's coat and briefcase were there, so he must be around somewhere. When he got back to the entrance, Geordie came through from the room opposite and greeted them.

"Good morning. Let me take your coats. The Reverend and her man are up in the nursery getting things ready. She wants to begin at sunrise, and it's almost that now. I have strict instructions to bring you up right away."

They made their way through the dining hall toward the staircase that led to the nursery. Helen felt a pressure bearing down upon her shoulders as soon as they mounted the stairs. It was the same sensation as the other times she had been there. She braced herself and continued up the worn stone steps, each step more difficult than the last. The higher she climbed, the heavier her feet felt.

"Bloody hell, it's happening to me again," she muttered. "It's like I can barely lift my feet, and I feel like there's a ton of bricks on my back."

"You are most certainly connected to our invisible inhabitants," noted Geordie, looking up at her as he followed behind. "Every once in awhile a visitor will tell me about an oppressive, weighty feeling they get whilst in the castle. Apparently it happens to those who have the ability to connect with those who have passed on, whether or not they have ever done so. It has never been an issue for me, personally, but I have had some staff quit because they never felt right while they were in the castle, and it frightened them out of their wits."

"Given my experiences here, I guess that's probably true – whether I like it or not," sighed Helen.

When they reached the top, they could see Reverend MacDougall in the nursery at the end of the hall. Matt and Ian exchanged a look, and followed Helen and Geordie into the nursery.

"Good morning everyone; glad to see you; I am ready to begin. Come in and take your places here."

She smiled and shook their hands as they each entered the room.

"Gregor has helped me to prepare everything. He does not want to be in the room with us during the ceremony, so he will wait in the hall. Come in…come in….now I want to have you in certain places."

Gregor left for a bench in the hall, shaking his head and mumbling disapprovingly. Geordie closed the door behind him. Geordie opted to stay back beside the door, while Reverend MacDougall herded the other three to stand by the fireplace. A small table stood in front of the fireplace. It was covered in a white linen cloth from the church, and there was a silver bowl with water. A gleaming silver cross laid across the top of the bowl. Beside the bowl were a bible, two candlesticks with white candles and a silver lighter. The Reverend herself was dressed in her Sunday service robes with a long gold pendant crucifix. She handed each of them a sheet of paper. "This is the Baptismal Covenant – you have seen this quite recently at little Helen's baptism. I will need the three of you to respond where it is indicated – just as you did at her baptism, and to each light a candle when we are finished. I have adapted the Covenant to suit our purpose here today. First, I will start with an explanation of why we are here today. Secondly, I will follow with the Covenant. Finally, I will end with a blessing of the deceased. Are you quite ready?" She looked at each of them as they nodded. "All right. Let's begin."

"We are gathered here today at Crathes Castle in this nursery for a very important and holy purpose. While events of the past, at times have cast a dark shadow and sadness upon people who have lived here, we are here today to try to right some wrongs committed on innocents, and to give them the eternal peace that they deserve to have as God's children. I am here according to the tradition of Anam-cara, with Ian and Matthew Wallace, and Helen Brooks, to collectively provide friendship and support to the soul or souls here, as they leave their earthly ties and find peace with God for eternity. We are here for this sole purpose this morning, as a new day begins for lost souls on their journey to be with the Lord. Let us begin with a Baptismal Covenant to claim the child and any others here as children of God."

With these words, Reverend MacDougall began the Covenant with Helen, Matt and Ian responding, reading the excerpts as indicated on the sheets she had given to them. As she came to the end, she picked up the cross from the bowl on the table and laid it on the hearth of the fireplace. While she did this, Ian, Helen and Matt each lit one of the candles, in turn, with the silver lighter. Reverend MacDougall then picked up the silver bowl and dipping her fingers into the bowl, marked the centre of the hearth with a watery cross.

"With this holy water, I baptize you, dear child, in the name of the Father, and of the Son, and of the Holy Spirit, and bestow upon the hearth a blessing, as the final resting place of one of God's innocent children. May peace be with you, and with this house, and with all who have lived here, who live or work here now, or visit. God, bless this hearth, and this house, and all the souls within it, past and present."

Reverend MacDougall took the cross from the hearth and held it up above her head.

"Now, we will ask a special blessing for the child's soul whom we believe to be here, and ask that it be guided to eternal peace away from earthly ties. Let us pray. 'Lord Jesus, our redeemer, you willingly gave yourself up to death, so that all might be saved and pass from death to life. By dying you unlocked the gates of life for all those who believe in you. So we commend this child into your arms of mercy, believing that, with sins forgiven, this soul will share a place of happiness, light and peace in the kingdom of your glory forever.'"

The Reverend lowered her arms and the others looked up. As they did the sun rose and light streamed into the room. Helen noticed some movement across the room and turned her head. There was the ghost of the young woman in the green dress and she was holding her arms out and looking toward the fireplace.

"She's here…the mother," whispered Helen, looking around at the others to see if they could see her too. "Can you see her? She is there by the window."

Helen pointed to where the ghost was standing. Ian nodded, transfixed by the vision in front of him. They turned their heads to look, but neither Matt nor the Reverend could see her.

"No, Helen, I do not see her, but I will continue," said Reverend MacDougall, holding the cross over the hearth of the fireplace. She bowed her head and began to pray.

"Christ Jesus, most merciful Saviour, Hear our prayers as we gather in Your Name We commend this child into Your arms of mercy. May the angels surround this child and its mother and the saints welcome this child with joy. Lord God, we commend this child to Your everlasting care. In the name of the Father, Son and Holy Spirit. Amen."

As she spoke these words, the light coming through the window grew brighter and brighter. Helen watched as the ghostly hands of a small child of about two or three, rose out of the hearth of the fireplace, followed by its arms, head; soon its shoulders appeared, then by the rest of its little body and legs. The child stood up, and looked up at the ghost of the woman by the window, cried 'mamma' and walked quickly over to her and into her arms. She picked up the child, and the light intensified into a white glow that shone through the window. The woman cradled her child, looking over at Helen. She smiled, said thank you, then turned and slowly disappeared with her child into the radiant glow of the light. After a few seconds, the bright light dimmed to rays of morning sunshine.

"They are gone," murmured Helen, trembling, "... into the light. Both she and her child. Did you see the child come up from the hearth?" Helen could hardly get the words out. She began to shake, and her knees felt as if they would give way. Matt and Ian moved closer to hold her upright.

"I saw them, Helen," said Ian softly. "They must be at peace now. " No one spoke or moved for several minutes, after which the Reverend began to gather her things together.

"Thank you, Reverend MacDougall. Thank you so much. I feel so light. And happy," added Helen. The pressure on her shoulders was gone and she felt normal again.

Matt smiled and hugged Helen. He was relieved to see that she was visibly okay, despite what she had witnessed.

"You are very welcome, my dear. I must thank you too. It is a humbling experience to be able to assist lost souls on their way – whether it be in the present, or the life beyond. I could not witness for myself what you and Ian have seen, but it was obvious that you both were transfixed on something from the expressions on your faces. I am so happy that the poor bairn has left its terrible grave, and is finally with its mother and God. It gives me great peace to know that."

She blew out the flames on the three candles. "Now, will someone fetch Gregor to help me? We will meet you downstairs."

Geordie went to get Gregor, who had fallen asleep on the bench in the hall, while Ian, Matt and Helen started down the staircase. Helen felt so light that it was as if she was floating down the long, winding steps. The three of them were in a kind of daze, struggling to fully comprehend what they had witnessed. There was also a sense of validation for having gotten it right. They got their coats and waited in silence in the front hall. Helen felt a stillness within, and appreciated the sudden absence of the anxious stomach pain that had plagued her for the past few weeks. She glanced at Matt who was looking at her and smiled as their eyes met.

"You were right, Lenny, you were right. Well done," he whispered.

Helen smiled back while tears suddenly sprang to her eyes and rolled down her cheeks. She choked back a sob, but then could no longer hold it in and began to cry, her shoulders shaking.

"Oh lassie, dunna cry. There there." Matt quickly encircled her with his arms and drew her close, her head resting on his chest. He looked at Ian who was looking rather pale and emotional himself.

"Are you okay brother? You look as if you've seen a ghost."

Matt uttered the latter slowly, hoping that some humour might lighten the situation. It did. Helen looked across at Ian's startled countenance at Matt's remark and couldn't help herself. She began to giggle, and then laugh until tears were again running down her face. At first, Ian was taken aback at his brother's words; however, once Helen began to giggle, he started to as well, and ended up in the same state as her, almost doubled over with laughter. It was one of those situations where laughter cannot be controlled and has to run its course until the body is fully exhausted. This happened within a few minutes, and Matt chuckled to see the two scholars had so completely lost control of themselves. When it was over, the two sat down, gasping and wiping their eyes, and trying to compose themselves. Both felt tremendously better, albeit completely emotionally spent.

"You certainly have a way with words, Matt," said Ian, "At first I couldn't believe you actually said that, but I couldn't stop myself when Helen started to laugh."

"Me as well," chimed in Helen, "it is a perfect ending to the absurdity of it all. It is a beautiful absurdity, though," she added wistfully, "I will never forget the looks on their faces – the mother and child reunited – they were so happy. And she said thank you – did you see that Ian? I couldn't hear her voice, but I could see the words on her lips."

"Aye, Helen, I saw. They are finally together, and at peace as they should be. It's been a good day so far. A very good day. One that I will never forget."

Ian stood up again and walked over to give the two others a hug. They could hear Geordie, Reverend MacDougall and Gregor as they neared the bottom of the staircase. They helped Gregor pack the Reverend's car, and thanked her again, waving gingerly as Gregor drove off. They thanked Geordie again, and left him smiling and waving at them from the entrance. Ian was eager to get home and to tell Sarah about everything. And to have a drink of whisky. A very large drink of a very good whisky.

Chapter 17 – A Pleasant Surprise

Sarah was waiting anxiously for them when they arrived home. She was relieved to see that the three of them looked unscathed, although tired, when they came into the house. "I'll put on a fresh pot of coffee – you must need it." They hung their coats up and followed her into the kitchen.

"We're in need of something a might stronger to start with, darling." Ian disappeared into his study and came back with a bottle of whisky. "I've been saving this for a special occasion, and I think this is it." He winked at Sarah as she went into the dining room and came back with three crystal glasses.

"Okay, but I'll make some coffee anyway. Thank you, but not for me, dear," she smiled, looking at Ian, "I will abstain, but you three go ahead. You all look completely done in. What happened out there?"

They sat down at the table and Ian poured them each a large whisky, neat. Ian and Matt drank theirs down immediately, and Ian poured them each another.

"It went as well as could possibly be imagined, Sari," said Helen softly, sipping at her whisky, appreciative of the smoky flavour, followed by the gradual warmth of her muscles relaxing. "Reverend MacDougall, bless her heart, had everything prepared when we arrived and performed the most beautiful blessing at the hearth in the nursery. It was really special. The ghost in the green dress appeared, and so did her child – right out of the hearth! It was the most astonishing thing that I have ever witnessed. Ian saw them too. They are together now, and they left into the most brilliant light that I have ever seen. They are at peace." Helen's eyes filled with tears recalling the image of the two going into the light.

"Oh Lenny, I'm so happy for you –and them- and so relieved."

Sarah leaned over and hugged her friend closely, kissing her cheek and smoothing Helen's hair back from her face as she might with a child. Helen gave a full account of the blessing ceremony, and of what she and Ian had witnessed.

"You see? You were definitely right to do this, and you have done a very good deed. You all have. And the Reverend- the dear woman. We are indebted to her, Ian – really. She has gone above and beyond. I think that maybe we should really make a bit more of an effort at the church. Now, Ian, that's enough whisky." Sarah interjected, chuckling as Ian reached for the bottle. " Let me get you all some coffee. I have to take the boys to school shortly. Why don't I drop you at the university, Ian, I want to talk to you about something anyway?"

Sarah was pleased when Ian nodded in agreement. Practical as ever, she thought it best to get back to normal as soon as possible.

"Why don't you and Matt relax here, Lenny, and we will celebrate properly this evening."

Sarah winked at the two of them and Helen blushed, knowing that she was deliberately giving them some time alone. She wondered what Sarah wanted to discuss with Ian alone. She hoped it had something to do with Sarah's resuming her research.

"That sounds like a splendid idea," added Matt, content with the proposal. "That coffee smells divine – no pun intended this time."

Helen and Ian laughed, and had to explain to Sarah about their respective emotional meltdowns after the ceremony, triggered by Matt's earlier remark. Sarah laughed with them and patted Matt on the back, congratulating him for his wicked sense of humour.

Ian and Sarah bundled the boys into the car and drove away. Helen had offered to look after the baby, so they left Helen and Matt at the kitchen table drinking coffee, with baby Helen babbling up at them from her playpen. It was a picture of domesticity that Sarah was pleased with – three of her most loved enjoying each other's company. It was no secret any longer that she was hoping for more than friendship between Matt and Helen. However, for the time being, she had to focus on her discussion with Ian and hope for the outcome she wanted there as well. After they dropped the boys off at school, Ian turned to her and asked her what was on her mind. He appreciated that she was driving him to work. He couldn't afford to take the day off with all of the extra administrative work he had to do, and he certainly couldn't have driven after a couple of whiskyes. He was glad that she had stopped him at two.

"What is it, my love?" He was a bit concerned when she did not answer immediately. The thought crossed his mind that she might be contemplating a separation. Although, since Helen had been here, they had been getting along better and Sarah had seemed happier. Maybe it was just that Helen was here, and as soon as she left, Sarah would be unhappy again, and she wanted to avoid that. He continued with these thoughts as he waited for her to speak.

"I want to resume my work – my research, Ian. It's been on my mind for a long time, but I was busy with the children and the house and everything. I know that won't change – I will still be busy with it all, but I really want to finish what I started – if I can." She glanced quickly at him and then back at the road.

"Oh, I see." He was somewhat relieved. "Well, I am surprised. I didn't know that you were thinking about it. You mean that you want to go back to Canada and finish there?"

Sarah shook her head, frowning. "No. I don't see how that could possibly work, with the boys at school and the baby's schedule. No, this is home, and, if I can, I want to finish my work here. That is where I need your advice, and help in approaching the university. I want to finish my doctoral work here at Aberdeen. I am hoping that you can help me with a proposal to the medical faculty."

"God, Sarah, you have no idea how relieved I am. I thought you might be thinking about leaving me. Not that I would blame you. I know that I haven't been a great husband, even a good husband for a long time –if ever."

She was stricken to hear him say this. She had no idea that he was even aware of how unhappy she had been feeling. She turned the car into the university grounds and parked in the lot beside his building.

"Ian, thank you for realizing that things have been a bit difficult for me. But I know it hasn't been easy for you at work either. And that's taken a toll on our family life. But, no, I don't want to be away from you. I love you and our family, and I want us to always be a family. So, it's important to me that both of us are able to balance our work with what's required on the homefront. I don't want the children to notice a huge change in their routines or parents' energy levels. That's the most important part."

She paused, giving his hand a squeeze. "Now, if you can help, I would like you to speak to Dr. Blake in the faculty of medicine to see if someone in the department would consider taking me on as a graduate student in the latter stages of research, with a view to finishing within two years. Given that I have already been away from it, on an active basis, for several years, he may not be too interested. The research is still relevant; I know that much; I have been keeping current with the developments in breast cancer prevention and treatment, and my area of focus would still be considered innovative. Helen thinks that it would help a great deal in contributing toward better cancer intervention methodology."

She looked to him for a response at this point. He had been staring down at his hands for most of the time, but he looked up at her and moved closer as he did so.

"Yes. Of course I will talk to Evan Blake about it. Frankly, I think he might be thrilled to have someone of your calibre in the department, and particularly with your specific area of concentration. I'll talk to him today after my meeting. Leave it with me, Sarah. I will support you fully with this, even though it will be a challenge with the children, but we can work it out. I can see that this is really important for you, and I do not see why we could not make it happen." Ian paused to think. " First things first; I will call Dr. Blake this morning and try to get a time to see him this afternoon. Sound good?"

He smiled at the shocked look on Sarah's face. He would have been right if he had thought that she expected resistance from him. If this would make her happy, and her life complete, then this is what they would do. Somehow. He hoped that Evan Blake would agree to think about it. He had known Evan for years and they had sat on a few committees together.

Sarah was almost giddy with excitement as she pulled up in the driveway at home. She couldn't wait to tell Helen the good news. The surprising news. She had expected some resistance from Ian, and perhaps some sulking. Although she fully expected that, if this were to materialize, there may indeed be some instances of sulking ahead. But nothing insurmountable. They would find a way to do it if, in fact, Dr. Blake agreed to take her on. Hopefully, the fact that he and Ian knew each other would work in her favour. If not, she would have to explore avenues for doing it at a distance, if her former Toronto faculty would agree to it. The lab work would be a challenge, in the latter case, however, and she wasn't sure how it might be worked out. *Best not to get ahead of myself until Blake renders an opinion on the feasibility of it. But Lenny will be pleased.*

She found Helen playing with the baby in the living room. She picked up the baby and cuddled her, then laid her back on her play blanket.

"Lenny, I have something to tell you." She sat down beside her friend, trying to look serious.

"Well, what is it, Sari? Is something wrong?" Helen couldn't quite make out whether Sarah was happy or not; her expression was somber, but something else was up given the twinkle in her eyes.

"Despite what's been going on with the Crathes blessing, I have been thinking a lot after what you said about picking up where I left off in my research. While you were gone to Crathes the first time, I went through all of my boxes and read through a lot of my work. To make it short and simple, I have decided to resume my research and finish my doctorate. That is, if it can be arranged with the University of Aberdeen." She relished the stunned look on Helen's face.

"Oh Sari! That's wonderful news! I'm so happy!"

Helen clapped her hands together, then hugged her friend. The baby looked at them and her tiny face broke into a big smile as she watched them.

"See, even baby approves! I am so thrilled and proud of you, Sari. But what does Ian think? Have you told him yet?"

"Yes, of course, Lenny, I talked to him about it this morning. I had to have his support before I could tell anyone else –even you, dear." She chuckled as she noted a flash of jealously cross her friend's face.

"Now, Lenny, don't be cross. Ian is my husband after all. Anyway, he is going to ask Dr. Evan Blake, who is head of the medical faculty at Aberdeen, whether he would consider asking someone to take me on as a grad student, to see me through my research and dissertation. He is going to try to see him today, Lenny, isn't it wonderful?" Helen could hardly believe that Ian was so immediately supportive of Sarah's wishes, although she was beginning to think that perhaps she had underestimated him all along. He did not seem to be the bad guy she had been convinced that he was for so many years. Their initial personality clash had sullied her impression of him and it had persisted. Now that she had gotten to know him, along with the fact that they seemed to have some things in common, however odd, had forced her to question her previous convictions about him. After all, he had been more than supportive to her during these past few tumultuous weeks.

"Wonderful is an understatement for what this is, Sari! This is fantastic news! I am so pleased for you. I really think that it is important to pursue your theory; I do believe that you were on to something very critical that might indeed provide a clue to more effective and less drastic treatments. Is there anything that I can do to help?"

Helen was thrilled with this news, and with how excited Sarah seemed at the prospect of finishing her work.

"Ian will have some news tonight, I hope," replied Sarah. "Let's see what he finds out and then we can go from there. Thank you, Lenny. If it wasn't for you, I probably would have given it up for good. Thanks for prodding me to do something about it." She hugged her friend and looked at her intently. "Now, are you sure that you are okay after this morning? I am pleased that everything transpired as we had all hoped that it would, but it must have been terribly frightening to see ghosts of the mother and the child."

"Strangely enough, Sari, I wasn't scared at all," Helen replied, pensively. "I don't know quite why because it certainly terrified me – at least the first time. To see her, and to see the child come out of the hearth is something that I will never forget. With any luck, I will not have this kind of experience again either! I have been thinking back to the dream I had that first night, and then the events that unfolded after that, and I can hardly believe it has happened. It's really kind of overshadowed our visit together, Sari. You and Ian, and Matty, have all been so supportive through it all. I don't know how I will make it up to you. I came to help you, and you ended up helping me – again." Helen sighed and leaned back into the cushions. Sarah scooped up the baby onto her lap.

"Lenny, don't be silly. You have been more help than you give yourself credit for. I couldn't have managed Helen's baptism without you and Matty, and it's been wonderful to have you both here. I could get used to it. And so could Ian. Yes, this blessing thing was unusual, I'll give you that, but it has certainly been an interesting process. Reverend MacDougall's reaction to it is what surprised me. Obviously this sort of thing is not as uncommon as we think. Especially in this country!" Helen nodded in agreement and appreciated Sarah's matter-of-face perspective on it all. As Sarah cradled her baby on the couch, rocking her and talking to her, Helen couldn't help but compare the sense of contentment and peace she felt now, with her feelings of that morning when she watched the ghost in the green dress, holding her child and walking peacefully into the intensely bright light.

Chapter 18 – Home With a Promise

Matt had offered to collect Ian from his office and the boys from their school and left Sarah and Helen where he found them talking by the fire. He was very pleased to hear about Sarah's wanting to resume her work, and he offered to help as much as he could with the children. Sarah looked relieved when he volunteered to drive into Aberdeen, and was more than happy to let him do it. Matt wanted a chance to speak with Ian and to explain the details of his upcoming trip to Toronto and New York. It was important to him that Ian understand that he would be coming back in several weeks, and that he had every intention to be true to his word and be a steady and reliable presence. He also wanted to enlighten his brother about his feelings for Helen. He didn't know where or if a serious relationship would manifest; however, his feelings for her were real and strong, and, for the first time, he really wanted to explore the possibilities of a serious relationship. Ian was waiting for him on campus and looked surprised, but pleased, to see him.

"This is a nice surprise, Matt," said Ian as he threw his briefcase into the back seat and got into the front. "I'm bushed. How was the rest of your day?"

"I had a wee kip, so I'm fine, Ian. The girls were having a good visit, so I thought I would offer to pick you and the boys up. I wanted to have some time alone with you anyway." Matt shifted in his seat as he maneuvered through the city traffic.

"Well, it seems that I am popular today. First Sarah and now you! What's on your mind?"

"It's my trip to Canada next week with Helen. She has graciously offered to host me in Toronto while I meet with these art dealers, and she may go with me to New York to meet the others. I wanted to explain it all to you – we kind of sprang it on you the other day, and I know it took you by surprise."

Matt paused as he focused on the traffic. Ian waited for him to continue, bracing himself for the inevitable news that Matt would be gone for quite awhile.

"I don't plan to be gone for too long; three to five weeks at most. I am going to be home, and I plan to make a nuisance of myself at your house. I meant what I said about being more reliable and helping out. Especially now with Sarah going back to her work. Yes, I know about it." He smiled at the look of surprise on Ian's face. "These meetings with the galleries are important, and I believe that my work will do well in both markets here and there. At least, I am assured that it will. But I must meet with the dealers at their galleries, and see them for myself. After things are set-up, everything can be managed from here with the occasional trip over."

Ian smiled as he listened, encouraged that Matt wanted to provide him with assurances as to his commitment to the family. It was a welcome development. Matt seemed genuinely excited about exploring this market for his paintings, and perhaps it was a good step for him to take. It seemed that this art thing had been working out pretty well for his brother in every way.

"And," Matt continued as they neared the hamlet where the boys went to school. "I think you should know that Helen and I have feelings for each other. It just kind of happened, Ian. I mean, I liked her right away, and she's lovely, but I realized when I went back to Edinburgh that I want to be more than just friends with her. Fortunately, she feels the same way."

He looked at Ian as he parked the car, wondering what his response was going to be given Ian's history with Helen. Ian was silent for a few moments. They got out of the car and walked to the school entrance to wait for the boys. Ian put his hand on his brother's shoulder and looked at him fondly.

"I thought it must be my imagination, because I thought you were a confirmed bachelor – wanting to enjoy the single life. I noticed how the two of you looked at each other, but with everything that has been going on – well – it's been pretty intense for us all. I am a bit surprised, but not entirely. I did wonder when you announced you would be flying home with her. I am surprised moreso with her than you – she's always been a bit of a loner. I'm pleased for you – for both of you. I hope it is the right thing for you both. But tread carefully, Matty, Helen is Sarah's friend, and I wouldn't want anyone to get hurt. Any of you. Well now, aside from that caution, this is good news. I like the idea!" Ian laughed, and hugged his brother.

They chatted about Matt's trip on the way home, and the boys were keen to hear about it too, insisting that their father take them to all the galleries to see their Uncle's paintings. The prospect of seeing their grandparents and Aunt Lenny again in Toronto was also foremost in their minds as they tried to convince their father. Matt encouraged them, much to Ian's chagrin, so he assured them that he would 'think about it and discuss it with their mother'.

Helen and Sarah had prepared a wonderful dinner of roast beef and Yorkshire pudding, with fresh vegetables, garlic mashed potatoes and thick, smooth gravy. Everyone was famished and they all sat around the table, even little Helen who chortled and laughed from her highchair. Betty had made a wonderful apple and pear crumble, and Helen had prepared a sticky toffee sauce to pour over the ice cream topping the crumble. The boys were ecstatic about their dessert and managed to cajole their Mom into giving them a second helping. They had great fun watching their baby sister's expression as she got her first little taste of ice cream.

With the weekend ahead, the boys were allowed to watch a movie, once they had bathed and gotten into their pajamas. Sarah and Helen put the baby to bed while Matt and Ian cleared the dishes and cleaned the kitchen. Later, with a roaring fire in the fireplace and glasses of red wine, the four relaxed in the afterglow of a wonderful meal and the warmth of the incomparable companionship of family.

"Sarah," ventured Ian, "I spoke to Evan Blake today and I have news. Can I share it now, or shall I wait until later." Sarah's eyes grew wide as she sat up and looked at him in anticipation.

"Now please. What did he say? What did he think?"

"He's interested. Very interested. He wants to meet with you on Monday – at your convenience. He gave me his e-mail and said just to go into his schedule to pick a time that works for you. And, he would also like to meet with Helen, before she goes, if possible."

"Really! He is interested! Helen – did you hear that? Oh my god, I can't believe it!" Sarah stood up and began to pace around the room.

"Sari, this is fantastic news! I knew it – of course he is interested! He would be an absolute pillock if he wasn't!"

Helen jumped up to join her friend, and the two of them hugged. Ian and Matt laughed at Helen's pronouncement. Nobody had better dare decline her Sari for anything she wanted – especially this. Then Helen stopped and looked at Ian.

"Why does he want to meet with me? Is there something I can do? Of course I'll do whatever I can. I know how promising Sari's work was, and necessary – to this day!"

"He wants to talk to you about filling a potential sabbatical spot at Aberdeen. One of his star professors is taking a two-year sabbatical, and he wants to explore the possibility of you filling in for her."

Ian was going to completely enjoy the reaction to this news. Sarah began to squeal with excitement and commenced jumping around the room. Helen was completely shocked, which was exactly what Ian hoped for while waiting for her response. She looked over at Matt, who was smiling like the Cheshire cat at this news.

"Oh, Lenny. Please think about it. Say 'yes' to it. It would be wonderful, and I am sure they would give you leave in Toronto." Sarah could hardly contain herself.

"Well. This is unexpected," said Helen, sitting down beside Matt again, and appreciative of the arm he put around her shoulders. "Of course I will think about it. And I will meet with Dr. Blake I will need to see exactly what they are doing and examine the synergies between the professor's work and mine. And the teaching – I will have to see what kind of schedule he has in mind. Yes, I will meet with him. It's an intriguing idea.

I would be able to spend more time with you, Sari, and the children. That would be wonderful."

All sorts of thoughts were going through Helen's mind. This was a surprising development.

"But more importantly, Sari, let's schedule your meeting with Dr. Blake, and you and I can look over your research this weekend, and make a plan for the meeting."

Sarah nodded in agreement, grateful for her friend's help to get ready. This would be one of the most important meetings of her life. She was absolutely thrilled at the prospect of having Helen nearby as she completed her work.

Later, as Helen lay in bed, thinking about the day and all that had transpired, she shook her head. *What a day! Such an incredible beginning, and such a surprising end. I must spend my last few days with the boys and the baby. And help Sari prepare for her meeting. And think about my meeting with Dr. Blake.* Helen felt entirely peaceful and calm, and happy, planning her final days in Scotland – especially with the possibility of coming back for a prolonged stay.

The prospect of spending time alone with Matt in Toronto and New York was also very exciting, and given the frenetic nature of the past few weeks, it would be nice to get to know him better under normal circumstances. She was more than fond of him, and eagerly anticipated the relatively unfamiliar waters of a serious relationship. *Everything is going to be fine*, she reassured herself, before she eventually fell into a deep sleep, calm and undisturbed.

About the Author

"Upon The Hearth A Blessing" is D. Berkana Tiwari's first novel. Recently retired, Dr. Tiwari was a senior federal government research and policy advisor, and executive communications strategist. She lives in Canada with her husband.